→ WESLEY ELLIS ←

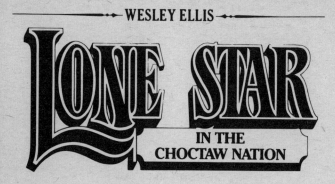

LONE STAR

IN THE
CHOCTAW NATION

JOVE BOOKS, NEW YORK

LONE STAR IN THE CHOCTAW NATION

A Jove Book / published by arrangement with
the author

PRINTING HISTORY
Jove edition / August 1991

ISBN: 0-515-10650-X

Jove Books are published by The Berkley Publishing Group,
200 Madison Avenue, New York, New York 10016.
The name "JOVE" and the "J" logo
are trademarks belonging to Jove Publications, Inc.

PRINTED IN THE UNITED STATES OF AMERICA

10 9 8 7 6 5 4 3 2 1

A SHOCKING CHALLENGE

"Let her go!" Ki yelled and threw the *shuriken*.

The man ducked, and the weapon went whistling over his head. He quickly drew the gun he had holstered, and he placed its barrel against Jessie's left temple. "You try that again, mister, and the lady dies," he growled, his eyes shifting swiftly back and forth between Ki and the deadly metal missile that had buried itself in the paneled wall of the coach.

Then he continued, "I'm getting out of here now, and the lady's coming with me. If you make another move like that last one, mister, she's a goner. I'll drill her. Then I'll drill you."

"Go ahead," Ki said calmly. "Drill her."

Jessie's eyes widened in surprise. She stopped struggling. Her lips worked, but no words came . . .

★

Chapter 1

The horse sunfished, almost throwing its rider. It sunfished a second time, its rider hanging on tightly and cursing colorfully.

"Ride him, Rusty!" called out one of the watching, unmounted men in the Starbuck cow camp.

The horse bucked, its rider's legs flying outward and upward before coming back down again, chap leather slapping smartly against the horse's sweaty hide.

"You take care, hear?" shouted Ki, the half-Oriental, half-Caucasian friend of Jessie Starbuck's, his hands cupped around his mouth in order to be heard. "Ride him, Rusty, or he's liable to wind up riding you!"

Ki's comments were followed by good-natured hoots of laughter and a few snickers.

Rusty wrestled with his horse, sawing on the reins and raking his horse's flanks with his sunburst spurs. The horse responded, not by calming down, but by bucking. Rusty's upper body was snapped violently forward and then as violently backward.

1

"Rusty, old boy, cut it out!" a man shouted. "You ain't no bird, so stop trying to fly!"

More laughter.

Rusty's hat flew off and went sailing through the air. He seized his horse's mane with his left hand and held the reins with the other while gripping his mount tightly with both legs in a desperate effort to remain in the saddle.

The horse shot up into the air and then came down on the ground with a loud pounding sound made by its hooves. Rusty let go of the animal's mane and clenched his fist. He raised it, and then, as his horse sunfished a third time, he sent his fist crashing down on the animal's skull.

The horse's head shot downward as a result of the well-placed blow. It snorted. Its knees buckled. It made an attempt to buck. Rusty responded by giving it another skull-splitting blow with his clenched fist.

When the horse stood stock-still, not moving so much as a muscle, Rusty grinned and raised his still-clenched fist in a gesture of triumph.

Too soon.

His horse suddenly lunged toward a locust tree that shaded the chuck wagon. It slammed up against the tree's trunk and began to try to scrape Rusty from its back. Rusty, taken by surprise by his mount's unexpected maneuver, let out a pained yelp and quickly pulled his left leg up. He hooked it around his saddle horn to prevent it from receiving any further injury and then quickly seized both of his horse's ears and twisted them as hard as he could.

The horse screamed. It shook its head but could not dislodge Rusty's hands from its ears, which he was still twisting, first one way and then the other.

The horse snorted. It gave another scream and then dropped its head. It did not buck. It did not try to scrape Rusty against the tree. It raised its tail and let a fragrant load of droppings fall to the ground.

"You done it, Rusty!" one of the hands crowed gleefully. "You cowed the son of a bitch for sure and certain, that's what you damn well did!"

Rusty grinned and stepped down from the saddle. "This old hammerhead of mine, he is about as ornery as a cat with

2

turpentine up its ass. Cain't figure him nohow and noway. One minute he's as peaceful as a church on a Saturday night and the next minute he's as cantankerous as a cook in a cow camp."

"Hey, now—"

"Present company excepted," Rusty quickly declared, giving the cook, whose protest he had just interrupted, a mocking bow.

"The joys of a life on the range," commented Ed Wright as he stood beside Ki. Rusty led his subdued mount over to the rope corral and wrangler that had been set up.

"I guess you've seen them all—the joys and the sorrows," Ki remarked. "You've been Jessie's ranch foreman now for how many years is it?"

"Too many to count." Ed smiled. "Well, that's not exactly true. Let's just say it's more years than I care to count, though I've begun feeling some of them in my bones come a rainy day."

Ki smiled.

He was tall for an Oriental, topping six feet. The skin of his face was smooth with few lines engraved on it, though it did show some small signs of weathering. His oriental heritage was most apparent in the epicanthic folds of his almond eyes. The fact that Caucasian blood, inherited from his father, also flowed in his veins was evident in the rest of his features, as well as in his height, which was greater than that of most pure-blooded Japanese. His blue-black hair hung down to his shoulders, straight and glossy.

"It's about time for me to be heading back to the ranch," he told Ed, handing the empty cup in his hand, which had held coffee, to the cook, who was busying himself at the chuck box.

"Tell Jessie everything's fine out here," Ed said. "No rain and no sign of rustlers. Two blessings I give thanks for every day neither one shows up."

"I'll tell her." Ki left Ed and went to his roan, which he had left ground-hitched on the eastern edge of the cow camp. He swung into the saddle and moved out, heading back to the Starbuck ranch and his friend Jessie.

As he rode, shadows were taking possession of the land

3

because the sun had dropped down out of sight, although there was still some light—shades of red and orange—tinting the western sky just above the horizon. Ki had not gone very far when the light faded and gave way first to evening, then to night.

His thoughts wandered as he rode through the darkness. He was once again in Japan working for Jessie's father, Alex Starbuck. Those had been good days. His employer had not ever given any sign of discrimination against his employee, as had many Japanese because of the fact that Ki was not a full-blooded Japanese. Alex Starbuck had always been fair and a friend as well as an employer. When it came time for him to return to the United States, his business in Japan successfully concluded, Ki was surprised—and altogether delighted—to be asked by his employer to come to America with him. He had gladly done so and had never had a moment's regret concerning his decision. He became good friends with the daughter of his employer, Jessica, and the two soon became inseparable. Now, thinking back over all the years—all the wonderful years of his close association with the Starbucks, father and daughter—he whispered a silent prayer of thanksgiving for his great good fortune. His only regret was the loss of his employer. Alex Starbuck's death had shattered him at the time, but he had eventually recovered, as had Jessie, who had also taken the event very hard. They comforted one another and helped one another endure the deep pain of their shared loss.

Ki heard the lowing of the cattle in the distance before he could see them. Mixed with the contented sounds they made as they settled down on their bedground for the night were the sounds of voices—men's voices. They were louder than the sounds of the cattle and getting louder as Ki rode closer to their source.

That would be Ace Crandall, the cowhand who had replaced Rusty as night herder, and Josh Pettigrew, another of Jessie's employees, who was also night-herding.

As the herd, most of them down on the ground, came into view, Ki also saw the two men and was able to make out some of their angry words.

Crandall: "Stay away from her or—"

Pettigrew: "Mind your own business, Ace."

4

As Ki came closer, he heard Crandall say, "She's my girl, and she don't want nothing to do with the likes of you."

"You're sure about that, are you? Well, I'm not. Kay Brent has a mind of her own, and she sure enough doesn't turn me away when I come calling on her."

Ki drew rein beneath the overhanging branches of a tall mesquite tree and, with his hands wrapped around his saddle horn, watched the two angry men confront one another. An age-old battle, he thought. Two bulls all riled up over a heifer.

"Get you down from up there," Crandall ordered as he slid out of his saddle.

"With pleasure." Pettigrew got off his horse and stood a few feet away from Crandall, his eyes glaring and his fists clenched at his sides. "If you want to fight, well, I'm willing."

Spunky little bantam rooster, Ki thought, watching Pettigrew, who weighed, he estimated, a good thirty pounds less than Ace Crandall and was a good foot-and-a-half shorter. The man was of slender build, unlike Crandall, who was built like a blockhouse, with shoulders as wide as an ox-yoke and a chest as big as a barrel. The man's got the weight, and it looks, Ki thought, like he's got the wind to go with it. Looks to me like Pettigrew's taken on maybe more than he can handle.

It was Crandall who struck the first blow—a roundhouse right that caught Pettigrew on the side of the head and sent him staggering dazedly to one side. Wasting no time, Crandall moved in on his opponent, both fists flying. He delivered a swift and savage series of blows, which landed on Pettigrew's chest and ribs. One of them buried itself in the man's gut, knocking the wind out of him.

Come on, Ki silently urged the man. Fight back. If you can't lick him, at least give him a run for his money.

Pettigrew, almost as if he were responding to Ki's silent commands, regained his balance and, with both fists raised, began cautiously to circle Crandall.

"Come on," Crandall taunted. "Try something, you sneaky little runt that's always creeping round the back door of the woman I mean to marry. Come *on!*"

As Pettigrew feinted, Crandall stepped nimbly out of his

5

reach. Pettigrew moved in, head low, fists up. His first blow struck Crandall on the chin, snapping his head backward and eliciting an enraged roar from the man. Pettigrew's second strike, a right cross, went off target, glancing off Crandall's left shoulder.

Neither hit did any damage. Crandall rushed forward. He seized Pettigrew in a bear hug and began to squeeze.

From where he was sitting his saddle, Ki could hear Pettigrew's breath gust noisily out of his lungs.

Pettigrew, straining as hard as he could, managed to break the larger man's hold on him. His arms flew upward, forcing Crandall's arms to the right and left. He lunged, his right fist hitting Crandall in the ribs. He let out a moan and shook his obviously hurt hand.

Go for the gut, Ki silently advised, not the ribs.

Crandall went down on the ground when Pettigrew, his face livid, lunged at him, head down, and butted him hard. Crandall had no sooner hit the ground than Pettigrew leaped on top of him and, straddling the downed man, began to throttle him.

Crandall's fists hammered Pettigrew's face and chest.

Pettigrew twisted his head and upper torso to one side to avoid the flurry of blows. As he did so, he shifted his center of gravity slightly, which caused him to lose his balance.

Crandall shoved him aside and then swiftly scrambled to his feet. Before Pettigrew could also regain his feet, Crandall kicked out at him, his thick-booted right foot slamming into the small of Pettigrew's back.

Pettigrew let out a howl of pain and fell facedown on the ground. Crandall went for him, seized him in both hands, and hauled him to his feet. He had barely done so when he thrust the man from him and kicked him in the buttocks, sending Pettigrew slamming into the thick trunk of a cottonwood.

Ki heard the sound of the collision and wondered, as the man slid down along the trunk of the tree to the ground, if any of Pettigrew's bones had been broken.

Pettigrew staggered to his feet and went after Crandall, who was standing, hands on hips, and laughing at his opponent, whose nose was now bloody and whose upper lip was split and oozing blood.

Pettigrew, breathing heavily, advanced on Crandall, his head lowered, his fists raised, his eyes on fire. Crandall, still laughing, stood his ground. Pettigrew threw a left hook, which missed Crandall but stopped his laughing. He interlocked the fingers of both his hands and brought them crashing down on the top of the shorter man's head.

Ki winced as Pettigrew slowly crumbled to the ground. First his legs bent. Then they began to tremble. Then they gave way on him and he slumped down on both knees. He started to rise but couldn't manage to do so. His head drooped until his chin was nearly touching his chest. His hands, no longer fisted, hung limply at his sides.

Crandall muttered an obscenity, a filthy name that he had applied to Pettigrew, which made the man wince. Then Crandall kicked him in the chest.

Pettigrew toppled over backward, a sibilant sigh escaping from between his lips. Not content with his apparent victory, Crandall moved in on Pettigrew and began to kick him, time after brutal time, in the ribs, the pelvis, the legs, the shoulders. Pettigrew rolled first one way and then the other, bunching his body, in a desperate but futile attempt to escape the savage punishment that was being inflicted upon him.

Ki leaped from the saddle and went racing toward the two men.

When he reached them, he seized Crandall by the shoulder with one hand and spun the man around to face him. Then his left arm shot out and the heel of his hand slammed into Crandall's chin, forcing the man's head backward. At the same time, his right leg flew up into the air and rammed forward. The ball of Ki's foot struck Crandall in the solar plexus.

A shocked grunt escaped from Crandall's lips as he staggered backward several steps, his angry eyes on Ki. He regained his balance and, cursing volubly, lunged at him. With his right fist he managed to land a glancing blow on Ki's left shoulder, but then he delivered a right cross that connected with Ki's jaw with skull-jarring force.

Ki danced backward, keeping his eyes on Crandall and moving to the left, then to the right, both hands open and raised, fingers pressed together. This time when Crandall came at him he took advantage of the man's stance—slightly bent

7

toward him as his hands reached out—to move in on the man. Maintaining a firm guard, with his left hand raised to deflect Crandall's inpending attack, he struck downward diagonally onto Crandall's beefy neck with a vertical chopping motion of his open right hand. His blow, as it was intended to do, stunned Crandall when it forcibly impacted on the large muscle in the man's neck.

The momentum of Crandall's lunge carried him still closer to Ki, who stepped back, marveling at the fact that the man was still coming toward him. He repeated his maneuver a second time, this time with far more force, determined not only to protect himself from Crandall's savagery, which bordered on sadism, but also to disable his attacker.

This time he was successful. He heard the sound of Crandall's collarbone snapping and saw the man's eyes widen first in surprise and then in pain.

Crandall's hands dropped to his sides. Then one rose to touch and quickly withdraw from the area of the broken bone. "Why, you—," Crandall began.

"Had enough?" Ki interrupted.

Crandall's answer was a roar of rage. Disregarding the injury inflicted on him, he once again made for Ki, his hands reaching, murder on his mind and showing plainly in his wild eyes.

Ki didn't move for several seconds as he judged the situation and decided upon his next maneuver. An instant before Crandall could touch him, Ki's hands flew to his sides as if in welcome and his left foot shot out and up, the ball of his foot colliding with the underside of Crandall's chin. Ki followed up with the same chopping strike he had just used on Crandall, breaking the man's collarbone on the opposite side of his neck.

Crandall seemed to shrink into himself. He wrapped his arms around his body and rocked slowly from side to side, whimpering softly, his head hanging down in abject defeat.

"Get out of here, Crandall," Ki ordered. "Go see Ed Wright back at the cow camp, draw your pay and ride out of here. If you can't get along with the men you work with, then it's high time you hit the trail."

"Where is it?" Crandall asked in a cracked voice.

Ki frowned. "Where is what?"

"The rock. The stone."

"What rock? What stone?"

"The one you used on me—twice."

Ki's frown faded. He almost smiled. "I didn't use any rock or stone. Just my hand. My open hand."

Crandall stared at him in disbelief.

"Move, Crandall. Get your horse and get going."

Crandall, moving gingerly and holding his body stiffly erect, went to his horse. He tried several times to climb into the saddle, but each time the pain apparently prevented him from doing so. Cursing under his breath, he grabbed his reins and began to walk, leading his horse.

When he had gone, Ki turned back to Josh Pettigrew, who was still on the ground, propped up on his elbows and staring wide-eyed with admiration at Ki.

"You okay, Josh?"

"More or less, I reckon, though I've got more aches and pains than a man could shake a stick at."

Ki went to him and helped him to his feet.

"You sure did do for Crandall, Ki. I never before saw anything at all like it, how you did for him. I never saw that kind of fighting before. Not in all my born days I didn't."

"I learned what I know about the martial arts, most of it, in the old country."

"China?"

Ki shook his head. "I was born in Japan."

"I'll tell you something. From what you say, if I ever run into somebody Japanese and he gets mad at me, I'm going to head for the hills and spend the rest of my life hiding out there and hoping he don't find me."

Ki matched Pettigrew's grin.

"I ought to have been born in the same place as you were, I reckon," Pettigrew went on.

"I'm afraid I don't understand."

"If I'd of been born in Japan, maybe I could have learned how to fight better than I know how to do the American way."

"That's not the point, Josh. The point is Crandall had height and weight on his side. You didn't have much of a chance from

9

the beginning going up against him. Come to think of it, why did you go up against him?"

"He told me in no uncertain terms to stay away from Kay Brent. I've been calling on her, but he said he'd already staked his claim to her and I was to butt out."

"I thought as much, judging by what I heard when I rode up."

"There's no way he was going to make me stay away from the woman I've fallen head over heels in love with. No way in the world."

Josh hesitated a moment and then continued. "Ki, I don't mean to impose on you or anything like that, but I was wondering . . . well, I thought maybe . . ."

"What's on your mind, Josh?" Ki inquired when the man fell silent and lowered his eyes.

"Watching you fight Crandall—the things you know how to do—well, I was thinking if I knew some of those moves, I might have been able to keep him from dragging me through a knothole the way he just did."

"I see. You want me to teach you the martial arts."

Josh looked up and eagerly nodded. "But I know you're busy—"

"Josh, a man can spend years learning the martial arts, which, incidentally, take many different forms and embody many different philosophies."

"Ki, I don't know a thing about philosophy or stuff like that. What I need to know is how to keep myself from getting whopped again."

"All right. I can teach you a few tricks of the trade, so to speak, that might come in handy for you some day in the future."

"Would you? When?"

"Right now, if you think you're up to it."

"Let's give it a go!"

"I'll show you how to do what I just did. The last two moves I made were called, in English, the Sword Hand and the Double Front Snap-Kick or *ago-geri* in Japanese, which means chin-kick."

Ki proceeded to demonstrate, in deliberately slow motion, the Sword Hand. "Watch," he told Josh, moving toward the

10

man with his hands raised, as if the cowhand were the enemy. "What you do is you keep your left hand raised—like this, see?"

Josh imitated his stance.

"That's good but not quite right. Your left hand should be higher. As if you were expecting an attack. That's better. Now, take your right hand—keep those fingers together—they're your weapon—and chop downward—like this."

Ki slowly brought his right hand down toward Josh's neck, his body shifting slightly to maintain his balance as he did so, but his feet never leaving the ground. His hand made contact—a feathery, fleshy touch—with Josh's neck.

"A blow of this kind will stun most any enemy. It will also—if you strike strongly enough—break his collarbone as I did in Crandall's case. Now you try it."

Ki coached Josh through the moves, guiding the man's hands with his own, positioning them, cautioning his pupil not to move too close to him, the "enemy," lest a counterattack foil his own attack.

"Do it again," he said when Josh had moved through the routine several times in slow motion.

Josh did, moving faster this time, his right hand streaking through the air. It landed on Ki's shoulder with great force.

"Easy, Josh," Ki cautioned. "This is practice. I don't want you to kill me."

"I'm sorry, Ki, I didn't realize what I was doing there for a minute. For a minute there, I thought you were Crandall and I wanted to kill you—him. Hell, I don't know what I'm saying."

"I do. And now is as good a time as any to point out something else a man who practices the ancient Japanese art of *Ninjutsu* should know."

"*Ninjutsu?*"

"That's the Japanese name for the martial arts practiced by the ancient—and modern—*Ninja* warriors. But let's get back to what I was saying. A *Ninja* warrior must keep his mind concentrated on what he is doing at all times. He cannot—dare not—let his mind wander as you admit yours just did. Such wandering could have dire consequences. Focus your mind on the task at hand. On your opponent. On victory."

11

Josh nodded.

"Do it again. More slowly this time."

The lesson continued with Ki teaching Josh the fine points of the *ago-geri*.

"Remember now, use the ball of your foot as the point of contact. And while you're about it, concentrate on maintaining your balance. It's no use learning how to deliver a high kick like the Double Front Snap-Kick unless you can stay steady on your feet to do so.

"And another thing. This is a move that can not only render an opponent unconscious but also kill him by snapping his head violently backward. So don't put too much force into it if you intend only to knock your man out, not kill him."

Josh performed the movements under Ki's watchful eyes several times, with Ki correcting the position of his feet and arms and the angle of his upraised foot.

"A move like this one is perfectly suited to following up with the Sword Hand as you saw me do with Crandall. Now what I want you to do is first kick and then chop."

Ki stood his ground to serve as "enemy" for Josh and was generally pleased with his pupil's performance.

"One other point of some importance," he told Josh. "If your kick should miss for any reason— -your opponent dodges or ducks, let's say—you can still overcome him."

"I can? How?"

"With the Sword Hand delivered once or twice as needed. Like this."

Ki demonstrated, talking his way through his moves, so that Josh would see and understand.

"You've missed with your kick. Okay. Bring your foot down fast like this. When it hits the ground, step forward. Now you've gained enough ground to reach the enemy's head. Now use the Sword Hand. Your forward momentum after your miss with the kick will give added weight to the blow you strike with your hand."

Josh tried it, simulating a missed kick. His follow-through— a sharp chopping blow of his hand—satisfied Ki, who congratulated his pupil on being what he called "a real fast learner."

Josh, obviously pleased, repeated the lesson several more

times until he was confident that he had mastered the moves completely. Then, with a glint in his eyes, he told Ki, "I feel like going after Crandall and giving him a little of what he gave me."

"A word of advice, if I may. Don't go looking for trouble. But if it comes, be ready for it."

"I'm no coward," Josh said, bristling.

"I'm not saying you are. All I'm saying is that it isn't cowardice to walk away from a fight. What that is is prudence. But you'll note that I'm also saying once you can't avoid a fight, jump into it and give it everything you have."

"What you've taught me today, it ought to stand me in good stead in most fistfights. But I wonder what I'd do in a situation where a man like Crandall was armed and came at me with a gun."

"Well, that's a whole other story. There's not a single answer to your question or single technique for dealing with a man with a gun when you've got none. First of all, you've got to take into consideration how far away he is from you. If he's close, you can shift your body fast. Like this."

Josh imitated the twisting movement Ki showed him.

"Or if he's a few feet away, you can parry his weapon like this. Farther away—step like this and then parry. If he's about medium range away from you, use a snap-kick like this to disarm him."

Ki illustrated the snap-kick and then said, "That'll knock the gun out of his hand nine times out of ten, and once you've done that, you can take him out with the other moves I showed you. Or," he grinned, "you can retrieve his weapon and shoot him with it."

"I'm not so sure I'd ever have the guts to go up against an armed man with just my hands—and feet—to use to defend myself."

"You might not at first, but if you practice what I've just shown you, it ought to build your confidence. Then, too, there's another way of looking at this thing."

"What's that?"

"Suppose a man throws down on you and you've not got a gun. What are you going to do? Just stand there meek as a mouse and let him gun you down?"

13

"That's a point, I've got to admit."

"You Americans have a saying. 'Nothing ventured, nothing gained.' In this case we're talking about, if nothing is ventured, what's gained is death or, at best, wounding.

"There are a few general rules to bear in mind when you're up against an armed man and you're weaponless except for your body and your brain. One: a moving target is harder to hit than a still one. Two: a small target is harder to hit than a large one. Three: it's harder to shoot a man who dives down and then rolls along the ground toward a gunman, than one who runs or jumps straight at him. Also, if your gunman is armed with a rifle instead of a side arm, that's an advantage for you."

"How so?"

"A rifle's less maneuverable in a hurry than a side arm is, which means you have a good chance of getting it away from him before he can shoot you. Keep out of range even when you're close to such a man. Crouch. Keep low. Run and weave at unpredictable speeds."

"But what do you do if he drills you?"

"If you're wounded and you stop moving or even just scream, he'll probably finish you off. You've got to continue to try to take him down. Chances are, if you're not too badly hurt, you can do it. Remember, if you don't keep on fighting, you're a goner. The man's out to kill you. If he wounds you, the advantage shifts to him—if you let it. Grit your teeth and keep after him. Disarm him any which way you can. There aren't any fair or unfair ways to play this game we're talking about and the only rule is to win any way you can, which, put another way, means to stay alive and to disable or eliminate your enemy.

"Keep in mind what some martial arts experts call 'the Wasp Principle.' The four letters stand for wisdom, accuracy, speed, and power. Wisdom's the controlling agent. Be alert. Miss nothing in your environment. Keep your mind keen. Watch for any advantage, and if there isn't any, make one for yourself. Physical skill or strength just aren't enough in weaponless defense against guns. Speed, accuracy, and power are important, granted. But it's the mind—wisdom—that overrides all three."

"I'm obliged to you, Ki. You've taught me more in a short time tonight than I learned in the two years I spent in the third

14

grade back in the Tennessee hills, and that's a true fact."

"I hope it'll help you if you get into another knuckle-duster like you did tonight."

"It's bound to, Ki, and I want to tell you I'm much obliged to you for taking the time to be my teacher tonight."

"Be seeing you, Josh."

Ki made his way to where his horse was chomping at some browse. He stepped into the saddle and rode out with a wave to Josh, who had also boarded his horse and was beginning to circle the bedded-down herd.

Ki rode through the starlit night, whistling as he went, enjoying the cool breeze that had begun to blow, stirring the limbs of the trees and bending the tall grass he was traveling through.

When he reached the ranch, he noted that only a single lamp burnt in one of the windows of the great room. She's not back yet, he thought, as he dismounted and led his horse into the barn, where he lighted a lantern. Maybe she decided to spend the night in town. He removed his gear from the roan and draped his saddle blanket over the wall of a stall to dry out.

He filled the stall's feed bin with a rich mixture of corn and oats, and then, as the horse hungrily ate, he rubbed it down until its coat shone in the yellow light of the lantern.

Carrying an oaken bucket, he went outside and filled it at the stone-walled well. Once back in the barn, he watered his horse and then left the animal to continue its feeding.

He was seated comfortably in the great room some time later and reading a copy of Charles Dickens's *A Tale of Two Cities*, which was bound in green morocco, when he heard the jingle of harness outside. He put the book down and went to the window. Drawing aside the lace curtain, he peered out.

There she was! His heart warmed as it always did when he caught sight of Jessie Starbuck after any separation from her, however brief it might have been. He went outside to where she was already unhitching her team.

"I thought you might have stayed over in town tonight when you weren't here when I got back," he told her, helping her with the harness.

"I got the supplies we needed," she said. "But I'm too bushed to unload them tonight."

"I'll do it for you."

15

"No, leave them, Ki. There's something I want to talk to you about. We can unload the wagon in the morning."

Ki helped her put the team away and then followed Jessie into the house. She seemed to him to be walking more slowly than usual. Was that due to the weariness she had mentioned? Or was he simply imagining a difference in her gait?

Jessie, emerging into the soft light of the lamp in the great room, seemed to glow. The light lent a softness to her features and even her skin. It made her green eyes gleam. It danced in her long coppery hair.

Jessie was slender but full-figured in the hips and breasts. Her waist was narrow without having to be cinched and her limbs—both legs and arms—were long and lean. There was a delicacy about her that at times hid the signs of her strong will and the equally strong resolve and determination that had made her one of the world's most successful businesswomen.

Ki, as she sat down—slumped down, really—into a high-backed leather chair studded with brass nails, took a seat opposite her, his book forgotten. He saw what he was sure were signs of strain around her eyes. She looked tired. But was a trip to town to do the weekly banking and to pick up a few needed supplies at the Feed and Grain sufficient to cause the signs of strain he saw in her face and body? There was, he noticed, the faint trace of a frown on her face as she sat with her arms hanging limply over the sides of her chair and stared across the room at nothing.

"Jessie, is something wrong?"

She didn't answer him. Not until he had repeated his question a second time. Then, "Yes, Ki, I'm very much afraid there is something wrong."

He waited, knowing that she would confide in him, that she would tell him what it was that was obviously bothering her.

She did a thoughtful moment later.

"I was passing the telegraph office and Orville Soames called out to me," she said, referring to the telegraph operator. "He had a message for me. It was from Luke Hodges."

Ki had to think for a moment before he could place the name. Then, "Luke Hodges," he repeated. "He's involved with Starbuck Enterprises' coal mining venture up north, isn't he?"

Jessie nodded. "He operates an open pit mine in an area

16

where our geologists found rich coal deposits last year in Choctaw Nation. He works under a lease arrangement, paying a per-ton royalty to Starbuck Enterprises on the coal he mines, as well as a royalty to the tribal treasury up there."

"What did he have to say?"

"He said there's trouble brewing between the Indians and the miners. He said there is talk of evicting the miners, who the Indians are choosing to call 'intruders,' from the Nation. I suspect such a threatened move is designed to pressure people like myself into hiking the royalty we pay to the tribe for the right to mine coal on their land. Luke also suggested that there are other potential sources of conflict coming to a head up there."

"Did he give you any details?"

"No, he didn't. But he did strongly suggest, if not exactly urge, that I would do well to make myself available to support him and his miners."

Ki said nothing as he watched Jessie carefully.

"I owe it to Luke and his men to help them in any way I can," Jessie said after a long moment of silence. "I'm also obligated to protect my own business interests that are at stake here. I plan to travel to Choctaw Nation to see what I can do to help resolve the problems Luke and his miners are confronting there."

"When?"

"Tomorrow. I plan to take the northbound train in the morning."

Already, he thought, Jessie looks less troubled. No doubt because she's made up her mind to act. Jessie always feels better when she is doing something. When she's actively involved in solving whatever problem is facing her or her business interests.

"I'll go with you."

"Oh, I don't expect you to do that, Ki. I know you've been planning on attending the barn dance at Ralph Kendrick's place this Saturday night."

"There'll be other barn dances."

"But you'll miss an excellent opportunity to continue courting the lovely Miss Lila Kendrick, Ralph's young and beautiful daughter."

17

Ki shrugged. "That's true. I'll just have to redouble my efforts in the courting arena with Lila once we get back. Maybe Lila and I will both benefit by my missing this Saturday's barn dance. You know what they say. 'Absence makes the heart grow fonder.'"

★

Chapter 2

The next day, Jessie stared critically at herself in the ornate gold-framed mirror in the beauty salon as the Missouri, Kansas, and Texas train sped northward.

"A little too severe, I think," she said to the woman who had been dressing her hair. "I think I look rather like a schoolmarm this way."

"Shall I loosen it up a bit then, mum?"

"Please do."

Jessie continued watching herself in the mirror as the hairdresser proceeded, with comb and brush, to fluff up her hair and create small springy ringlets that hung down on either side of her face. Twenty minutes later, Jessie expressed her satisfaction with the woman's earnest efforts and rose from the chair in front of the mirror. She paid the woman for her work, tipped her generously, and then, retrieving her reticule from the counter beneath the mirror, made her way out of the beauty salon.

A few minutes later, she found Ki in the library.

He looked up as she entered the coach and smiled. "You

look lovely, I must say. But then I thought you looked lovely before you decided you needed to have your hair done."

Jessie sat down beside him. "You'll turn my head with your flattery, sir. What are you reading?"

"*A Tale of Two Cities* by Charles Dickens. I was reading it at the ranch when you came home last night and was relieved to find that the train's library also had a copy, so I could find out what happens next."

"Mr. Dickens is a fascinating author. But I find his stories—parts of them—too sad for my taste. Like that one you're reading. I cried when I came to the part near the end that told how Sydney Carton—"

"Don't tell me!" Ki cried, holding up a hand to interrupt Jessie. "You'll spoil the suspense if you tell me."

"I won't say another word, I promise." Jessie looked around the coach, which was lined with shelves full of books and clouded with the cigar smoke of the men among the readers. "I'm hungry. Are you? Shall we get something to eat?"

"Now that is an idea I can readily go along with. While I was reading, I wasn't aware of how hungry I was. But now—I could eat enough for a battalion of men. Let's go."

Ki rose and, tucking the novel under one arm, offered Jessie his other one. They made their way out of the library and through two passenger coaches until they came to the dining car.

A waiter bowed them inside and showed them to a table that was covered with a sparkling white linen cloth. In the center of the table sat a crystal bud vase containing a single red rose.

The waiter handed Jessie and Ki each a large menu. He stood silently by, pencil poised over a notepad as they both studied their choices.

"I think I'll have the clams on the half-shell and the boiled California salmon with French peas," Jessie said a few moments later.

Ki looked up at the waiter and said, "I'll have green turtle soup and the antelope steak with orange fritters. May we see your wine list?"

"Certainly, sir." The waiter produced the list, and Ki perused it for several moments before ordering a white Bordeaux. When the waiter returned with it and opened the bottle, Ki watched the man partially fill a goblet with wine and place it before him. He picked it up, moved it back and forth in front of his nose, nodded his approval of the bouquet, and then tasted it. He nodded again and the waiter placed the bottle on the table and left.

Minutes later, he was back with their appetizers, which he placed before them. When the man had again gone, Ki filled Jessie's wineglass and his own and then raised his glass.

"A toast?" Jessie inquired. "To what, may I ask?"

"To the future. May it be happy as well as prosperous."

They drank.

"I'm not sure how happy—or prosperous—it will be in the coal mines outside of McAlester," she commented. She speared a clam, dipped it in the sauce the waiter had brought and ate it.

"You're worried," Ki said. A statement that was almost a question.

"I am. Oh, I know what you're going to say. Something about not crossing bridges until I get to them. But I can't help it. Luke Hodges's telegram sounded altogether gloomy. No, worse than that. Alarmed."

"There's a saying I heard spoken once—an American one, by the way, not one of my famous, if fictitious, Japanese proverbs."

Jessie smiled as she finished the last of her clams. "What is it?"

"'Of ten troubles you can see coming down the road, nine may never arrive.'"

Jessie nodded but then, pointing her fork at Ki, said, "All very well and true, I suppose. But what about that tenth trouble that *does* arrive?"

"The odds are still in a person's favor, according to the saying. Nine to one. Not bad odds at all, I'd say."

Jessie, as the waiter returned with their entrées, was silent.

"I don't recall you ever mentioning that you had trouble with your leased coal mine before," Ki remarked as he began to cut pieces from his antelope steak.

"We never did have any before. The Choctaws were glad to have us there because it meant a steady flow of money into

21

their tribal treasury in the form of the royalties we paid them. But there has been a lot of unrest in the Nations lately according to what I've read in the newspapers. The Five Civilized Tribes have come to resent the presence of white men in their homelands. They feel the whites are exploiting them and their land, so now I guess they've turned their anger against mine owners like myself. Up until now it had been, as I understand it, directed principally at two groups. One group was the Texas drovers passing through the Indians' lands and refusing to pay the per-head grazing fees the Indians imposed upon them. The other group was composed of Negroes who had drifted from Texas north into the Nations since the war ended."

"I'd heard about that second problem," Ki said. "A lot of the freedmen have been claiming to be citizens of the Nations so that they can gain all the privileges that such a status would bestow on them. But the Indians are claiming that there are four times as many Negroes in their territory as were ever held as slaves by them."

"There's no doubt in my mind that some of those Negroes are lying. They came up from Texas and are just trying to get a free ride from Choctaw and Chickasaw Nations and the rest of the tribes. I can readily understand the Indians' anger that's been directed at them."

"I never took you for a bigot, Jessie."

"Bigot? Me? I'm no bigot and you know it. But the Negroes I'm talking about are just more Texas trash that's drifted north. White or black, those kinds of men are just that—trash, in my opinion. Shiftless and no-account."

"I wonder if those Choctaws we're going to call on have a grudge against half-Japanese folk like myself," Ki said with a humorless smile.

"Those Choctaws aren't bigots either, and you know it. They're just trying to protect their own interests for the overall good of the tribe. I see nothing wrong with that."

"The way you talk—I'm not so sure you should be the one to try to help Luke Hodges with his problems, whatever they may be. You sound like a spokesperson for the Indians."

"I'll fight for my rights as I see them when I get there," Jessie said firmly. "You can count on that. After all, I signed an agreement with Chief Joseph Bryant, who was then and still is the Principal Chief of Choctaw Nation. I fully expect him to live up to the terms of that agreement, and I intend to see to it, in whatever way is necessary, that he does so."

Ki saw the fire flash in Jessie's eyes. He thought it was time to drop the subject. "This steak is delicious. How's the salmon?"

"Tender. Tasty."

Ki, as he continued eating, gazed out the window at the Texas landscape flowing by the train's windows. In the distance, a herd of pronghorn antelope went racing across the sun-parched prairie. He looked down at his plate, at the remains of the meat on it. This one, he thought, didn't make it in our dog-eat-dog world. Or, to be precise about it, in our man-eat-antelope world.

"What are you smiling at?" Jessie asked him.

"Oh, nothing. A crazy thought crossed my mind, that's all."

The waiter reappeared a few minutes later with the dessert menu. Jessie selected a chocolate mousse and coffee, but Ki ordered only tea.

"Oh, by the way," he said when their waiter had gone, "I forgot to tell you. I gave Ace Crandall his walking papers yesterday."

"Oh? Why?"

"He got into a fight with Josh Pettigrew and gave Josh a pretty bad beating. But that wasn't the only reason. Ace had been causing trouble of one kind or another among the men for some time. He's the kind of fellow who just can't seem to get along with other men. You put a fellow like Ace Crandall to work with a bunch of other men, and it's a little bit like putting a cat into a cage with a bunch of canaries."

"My hired hands can hardly be described as a bunch of canaries."

"Just a figure of speech. No need to get your dander up. All I'm trying to say is Crandall stirs up trouble wherever he goes, the way the wind stirs up dust. Neither he nor the wind can help it. What they do, it just comes natural to them."

"Is Josh all right?"

"He'll be pretty sore for a few days, no doubt. Crandall kicked him and did everything else to him except bite him, and I figured he would probably have done that, too, if I hadn't stepped in to cool things down."

"I wondered where you got that bruise over your left eye."

Ki raised a hand and gingerly fingered the bruise that had turned purple overnight and would, he knew, soon turn yellow. He was about to say something when the train suddenly slowed, its wheels screaming against the rails and sending up a shower of bright sparks outside the windows.

A woman dining at the rear of the car screamed as her chair flew out from under her and she toppled to the floor.

Jessie grabbed the edge of the table to keep from falling backward as Ki was thrown against the side of the coach, his left shoulder striking the grimy windowsill.

The sound of dishes falling to the floor and shattering was accompanied by cries of dismay and pain from startled and, in some cases, injured diners. One man sat dazedly on the floor in the middle of the aisle that ran through the center of the coach, blood oozing from a two-inch gash on his forehead. He had suffered the injury when he had been thrown to one side and his head smashed into and then through the windows next to his table.

Ki shot to his feet and pushed the table out of his way. "Are you hurt?" he asked Jessie.

"No, I don't think so. What happened?"

"I don't know. We must have hit something on the tracks. The train tried to slow down—and then there was the impact. I—"

Out of the corner of his eye, Ki caught sight of a mounted man riding past the coach windows. "Come on," he said to Jessie, taking her hand. "We're getting out of here. Do you have your gun?"

"Yes, in my reticule. Why?"

"Unless I miss my guess, we are about to receive a visit from some road agents."

"The train's being robbed?"

"Come on." Ki, taking Jessie by the hand, led her down the aisle, which was cluttered by broken dishes, cutlery, and shattered crystal and crowded with diners whose meals had been interrupted by the train's sudden stop.

They had almost reached the door at the end of the coach

when it flew open and a man wearing a striped bandanna over the lower half of his face and gripping a Smith and Wesson .45 in his huge hand yelled, "Stop!"

Ki and Jessie obeyed his order, halting in their tracks, their hands still linked.

"Everybody, listen up!" the gunman yelled. "See this here sack I've got?" He held up the gunnysack that was clutched in his left hand. "I'm going to give it to this gent standing right here next to me, and this gent, what he's going to do is he's going to put all his valuables into it and then when he's gone and done that he's going to pass the sack on to the next gent—that fat-faced fellow standing next to him—"

"See here, sir, you can't—"

"Shut up!" the gunman bellowed, his eyes, glittering above the upper rim of his cloth mask as he swung the barrel of his gun in the direction of the man who had just spoken.

A woman gave a strangled cry and then clapped both hands over her mouth as the gunman turned and glared at her.

"Like I was saying," he continued, "the next gent'll drop his valuables in the sack starting with that diamond stickpin he's wearing in his cravat, and then he'll pass the sack along. That's the order of business. You all understand it?"

People nodded. A woman whimpered.

The gunman handed the sack to the passenger standing next to him. The man took it, pulled his purse from his pocket, and dropped it into the sack. He handed the sack to the man next to him, who was now leaning weakly against the wall of the coach and perspiring heavily. That man removed his diamond stickpin and dropped it into the sack. The stickpin was followed by a garnet ring and then a thick billfold.

As the sack made its way from hand to hand toward where Jessie and Ki were standing, he released her hand and they exchanged glances. Then Ki's eyes dropped to the reticule in Jessie's hand. He looked up at her again, and something unspoken passed between them.

A moment later, the woman whose whimpers had turned to frightened sobs handed the gunnysack to Ki. He took it from her and reached for his gold watch, which rested in a pocket in his vest. He pulled it out by its chain, which was looped

25

across his vest, and then dropped it, together with its chain, into the sack.

As he did so, he seemed to stumble. But he quickly recovered his balance. The gunnysack in his hand was now directly in front of Jessie, and it did not waver as he removed his billfold from the inside pocket of his sack coat and dropped it into the cloth receptacle.

Having done so, he took a step backward and nodded to Jessie, and she reached into her reticule, a movement the gunman could not see because the gunnysack in Ki's hand hid her hand from view.

Without removing her double-barreled derringer from her reticule, Jessie fired.

Sound erupted in the coach. Women screamed. Men swore. The report of the round reverberated in the confined space.

The gunman went facedown on the floor of the coach, a red hole in his chest. Ki ran to him and placed two fingers on the side of the man's neck. He looked back at Jessie and said, "Dead."

The other passengers in the car stared at Jessie, some of them with awe in their eyes, others in abject fear as if she were going to turn her gun on them next.

Ki rose and handed the cloth sack contributed by the passengers to the man nearest him. "Take the other door," he called out to Jessie as he took up a position to the left of the door at the opposite end of the coach. "The sound of your shot might bring reinforcements."

"I'm getting out of here!" a man yelled and started pushing people out of his way as he headed for the door beside which Jessie had stationed herself. "I'm not getting caught in any crossfire!"

He never made it out the door. Even before he was halfway to it, another masked man burst into the coach brandishing a gun. "What happened in here?" he bellowed, his eyes darting from face to face as he surveyed the passengers.

Then he saw the body of the dead bandit lying in the aisle. "Who—"

He never got to finish his question. Jessie slammed the butt of her derringer down on the side of his head. He let out a sibilant sigh and fell unconscious to the floor of the coach.

26

"Give me your belt!"

"What?" spluttered the man Jessie had addressed.

"Your belt. Give it to me. Quickly!"

The man fumbled with his belt, and then, sliding it through the loops of his trousers, he handed it to Jessie. She used it to tie the downed gunman's hands behind his back. When she had done so, she picked up the gun he had dropped when he fell and rose to find that Ki had disappeared. She cautiously opened the door behind her but saw no one. She left the coach she was in and entered the adjoining one, the dead man's gun in one hand, her derringer in the other. The coach, she discovered, contained only two passengers—a woman and the baby she was holding in her arms. The woman was softly weeping as she rocked the baby, who gurgled and cooed as it gazed up at her. Seeing Jessie, the woman said, "They took it. My wedding ring. It was all I had to remember my dead husband, Isaiah, by. We never could afford to have pictures taken when he was alive. Now it's gone." Her weeping intensified as Jessie bent down and peered out a window.

Two more road agents were outside the coach. So was a crowd of passengers, the men standing with their arms straight up in the air, alarmed looks on their faces.

Jessie raced down the aisle to the door and went through it. Once out in the small space between the two coaches, she chanced a glance around the edge of the coach she had just left. Nothing had changed. One of the two gunmen was moving among the passengers with a gunnysack in his hand, collecting valuables while his confederate stood guard over the victims being robbed.

Jessie drew a deep breath and then jumped down to the ground, her derringer in her left hand and in the other, the gun that had belonged to the road agent she had knocked senseless.

"Hold it!" she shouted.

Both gunmen turned in her direction.

"Drop those guns!" she ordered. "*Now!*"

Both gunmen fired at her. One of their rounds buried itself in the side of the coach; the other pinged off the iron railing running up the side of the coach.

Jessie promptly returned the fire, but she, like the two road agents, missed her target—the gunman with the sack in his hand.

She ducked back between the two coaches—and felt the menacing barrel of a gun ram itself into the small of her back.

"Such a brave little lady!" a man behind her snarled, a man she could not see. "But a foolish little lady as well. Drop your guns, missy."

Jessie had no choice but to obey the barked order. She dropped both guns on the ground.

"Now, march!"

She stepped down from between the coaches and marched. When she reached the assembled crowd of passengers, she halted and turned around to face the man who had taken her by surprise.

His eyes, she noted, had a frantic look in them. They looked crazed to her. Dangerous. She imagined that beneath his mask he was grinning as he stared at her.

"Whatcha got there?" one of the other two gunmen asked him.

"A filly that busted out of her stall and got herself into a mess of trouble, that's what," was the answer. "How are you two doing?"

"We're just about done doing here," one of the men replied.

"We've got a sackful of stuff," the other said. "Jewels, gold, money galore!"

"Where are the others?"

"Inside the coaches," one of the pair answered.

"I'll be back shortly," said the road agent who had taken Jessie prisoner, as he dropped a hard hand on her shoulder.

"Where're you going?" one of his confederates asked.

"Inside the train."

"With the woman?" A snicker.

"Yes, with the woman."

"What you fixing to do to her once you get her where you want her?" Another snicker.

"You keep this bunch out here under control until I get back, hear?"

"Do I get a crack at sloppy seconds when you're through with her?"

"That's okay with me," the gunman said as he shoved Jessie ahead of him and then forced her to climb up and enter one of the empty coaches.

Ki lay flat on top of the coach onto which he had climbed after Jessie's run-in with the road agents in the dining car. From his prone position, he could see the two gunmen, who were continuing the process of relieving the passengers of their valuables, but could not be seen by them. He had heard the exchange of shots between Jessie and the gunmen below him, and he had seen her taken into the coach by the third road agent.

He hesitated, wondering if a change in plans was called for. He had not expected Jessie to be taken prisoner. Should he now try to rescue her from the road agent—who had taken her into the coach for a purpose that was all to clear to Ki but one he would rather not think about—or should he stick to his original plan to take out the two road agents below him?

"The tiger can kill the elephant not by a frontal attack but by dropping down upon it from a tree and biting it to death, bit by bit."

The adage echoed in Ki's mind. It was one he had been taught in the *sensei* in Japan many years ago by the young but very wise man who had also taught him the martial arts.

He would, then, be a tiger. Jessie's life, he believed, was not in danger, although he knew her virtue most certainly was. The people below him—should any of them resist the efforts of the gunman who was taking their valuables from them—might well die with a bullet in their bodies or brains. Ki reached into his vest pocket, and his fingers came to rest on the several cool metal *shuriken* he kept there. He slid from his pocket one of the five-pointed stars with the double-edged blade on each of its five points. His finger slid across the pintle hole in the *shuriken* as he fitted it to his fingers and then shot up into a crouching position.

The *shuriken* flew from his hand and went spinning through the air, catching the sun and glinting in its light, to strike and lodge in the gunhand of the man who was guarding the cowed passengers.

The road agent let out a cry of pain as he dropped his gun

29

and seized his right hand with his left. He shook his hurt hand and the *shuriken* fell from it.

"What the hell—," his companion exclaimed as he turned and saw Ki, who was now standing, another *shuriken* in his hand, on top of the coach. He said no more. Instead, he took aim at Ki and fired.

An instant before the round was fired, Ki sent the deadly missile in his hand spinning toward the gunman, and before the round the man had fired could reach him, he dropped down again upon the roof of the coach. As the shot screamed over his head, he looked up to see the man who had tried to kill him standing with his arms akimbo and a startled expression on his suddenly pale face.

From the center of the road agent's forehead protruded two of the *shuriken*'s five sharp blades. The other three had penetrated the man's skull and bitten into his brain. As Ki watched, the man's body seemed to turn to water. It flowed down to the ground and lay there in a twisted heap, lifeless and now forever silent.

"*Don't!*" Ki shouted to the dead man's companion, who was reaching for the gun he had dropped with his uninjured left hand. The man froze. Straightened. Stared up at Ki and at the glinting *shuriken* in his hand.

"Some of you men," Ki called out, "get their guns and tie that man up. Use a belt or suspenders—something. Stand guard over him and shoot anybody else who might show up."

Only when Ki was sure that his order was being carried out did he climb quickly down the ladder on the side of the coach, the *shuriken* still in his hand. A moment later, he burst into the coach, ready for the worst.

"Ki!" Jessie cried when she saw him. She continued struggling with the masked bandit in an attempt to free herself from his firm grip.

"Let her go!" Ki yelled and threw the *shuriken*.

The man ducked, and the weapon went whistling over his head. He quickly drew the gun he had holstered, and he placed its barrel against Jessie's left temple. "You try that again, mister, and the lady dies," he growled, his eyes shifting swiftly back and forth between Ki and the deadly metal missile that had buried itself in the paneled wall of the coach.

Then he continued, "I'm getting out of here now, and the lady's coming with me. If you make another move like that last one, mister, she's a goner. I'll drill her. Then I'll drill you."

"Go ahead," Ki said calmly. "Drill her."

Jessie's eyes widened in surprise. She stopped struggling. Her lips worked, but no words came.

Ki took a step toward the gunman.

"Get back!" the man screeched nervously, sweat glistening on his forehead.

Ki took another step toward him. "If you shoot her," he said tonelessly, "you won't have any way to keep me from coming after you. You'll have to bet your life on the fact that you can shoot faster than I can move and get my hands on you. Are you by any chance a gambling man?"

Ki, watching the masked man closely, saw his hand tremble and his eyes blink, both clear signals of his uncertainty. Ki wasted no time. He moved forward swiftly, his eyes shifting to Jessie, who read the silent message in them and kicked backward with her right foot, striking the gunman on the shin with the heel of her shoe.

The road agent let out a yell and raised his leg. As he did so, Jessie broke free of him and ran past the still-advancing Ki, who seized the wrist of the man's gunhand and twisted it. The gun fell to the floor of the coach.

Jessie retrieved it and leveled it at the road agent.

Grimacing because of the pain in his leg that her strategically placed kick had given him, he raised his hands while simultaneously uttering a gross oath.

"Outside," Ki ordered, releasing his hold on the man's wrist and retrieving the gun he had dropped.

The man, muttering unintelligibly now, moved to the door of the coach, glancing from one gun to the other in the hands of the pair who had gotten the drop on him.

They followed him outside and marched him over to where the crowd was gathered around the road agent lying on the ground, whom the men had tied with two pairs of suspenders around his hands and an equal number of belts around his ankles.

"He's not going anywhere," Ki said. And then, "Are you all right, Jessie?"

31

"I'm fine. A bit unsettled—but fine." She surveyed the area and then glanced at the train. "Have we got them all, do you think?"

"I think so. But keep your eyes open in case there's a stray we missed." Ki turned his attention to the crowd of men. "There's a dead man in that coach there." He pointed to it. "There's also a live one under guard. Some of you men, go get both of them and lock them in the caboose along with this one here."

He watched with Jessie then as his orders were carried out and the conductor of the train hurried up to him, slapped him on the back, and declared, "Marvelous job you two did, sir. Simply marvelous. You and the lady both deserve a great deal of credit. Had you not come to our aid so bravely, so fearlessly—"

"Thank you," Jessie said, interrupting the man's enthusiastic monologue before he could turn and slap her on the back as well. "What happened?"

"You mean what happened to the train? We rounded that bluff up there," the conductor pointed to it, "and there was a huge pile of trees and boulders on the tracks. You can't see it from here, but it's there. The engineer put on the brakes, but it was too late. We plowed right into it. We bent the cow-catcher rather badly, I'm afraid. Then the road agents were upon us before we knew really quite what had happened. A most regrettable incident. But all's well that ends well, as they say."

As if to punctuate his remarks, the caboose door slammed shut and the men who had placed within it the road agents, those alive and those dead, barred it.

Ki beckoned to them. When they had joined him, he said, "We've got a job to do up there around that bluff." He told them about the obstruction that had been used to stop the train.

"We've got to remove the debris before we can be on our way again," he explained. "I'll need some volunteers to help me and the train crew to do that. How many of you are willing to lend a hand?"

A score of hands went up.

"Will we be able to resume our journey once the track is

cleared?" an anxious matron inquired. "My husband's waiting for me at the next station, and I'm sure he'll be terribly worried now that we're so late in arriving."

"We'll manage, ma'am," the conductor assured her as the men who had volunteered headed for the bluff and what lay around it.

"I'm going to help clear the tracks, Jessie," Ki said.

"You gave me the fright of my life a little while ago," she remarked as she retrieved the derringer she had been forced to drop earlier. "I suppose you know that."

"You mean when I told that road agent to drill you if he was so bound and determined to do so?"

Indignantly: "That's exactly what I mean."

"I was sure he wouldn't do it. Not when I pointed out to him that if he did he would have played his high card and then the game—for him—would have been over."

"Oh."

"By the way, we make quite a team, don't you think? All I had to do was give you a quick look and you knew when to make your move, which brought the game to a fast end in there."

"All I can say at this point is that I'm glad it's over and we're still in one piece. I—"

The woman Jessie had met in the coach earlier with her baby came hurrying up to them, a broad smile on her face and her infant in one arm. "Look!" she cried, holding up her right hand on which a gold wedding band gleamed. "I got my ring back. The men distributed everything that had been taken from us and—oh, I'm ever so grateful to you both. This wedding ring of mine—it means ever so much to me."

When the woman had gone, Ki said, "I'd better get my billfold back."

As he was about to leave, Jessie said, "I hadn't expected to run into any trouble until we got to McAlester."

Ki smiled. "What happened here—let's call it the appetizer. The main course is waiting for us up in Choctaw Nation."

Jessie tried a smile that didn't quite work.

★

Chapter 3

The train, three hours late, finally pulled into the station at McAlester with a shriek of its whistle and a geyser of smoke from its stack.

Inside their coach, Ki was on his feet taking his and Jessie's luggage down from the overhead rack.

He followed her up the aisle and out onto the wooden platform, where a cloud of ash and an occasional ember showered down upon them.

"It's a wonder this platform—and others like it—don't go up in smoke," Jessie remarked, stamping out an ember that had eaten into one of the platform's wooden boards, which was sending up a thin tendril of gray smoke.

"It's a wonder the passengers don't go up in smoke—at least some of them," Ki said as he slapped away the ash that was dusting his clothes.

"The hotel's up that way," Jessie said, pointing to a wide street that ran at a right angle to the station. "It's not far."

Ki, carrying most of their luggage, except for a small carpet-bag Jessie had in her hand, began to trudge up the street past shops and people entering and leaving them. His eye was caught by a big-bosomed blond woman with hips like balloons, who, he thought, had smiled at him. Maybe even winked. Or was that all wishful thinking on his part? He wondered if McAlester boasted a whorehouse among its business establishments. He saw no red trainman's lantern hanging outside any of the houses he glimpsed lining the intersecting side streets, which was not encouraging. But his hopes weren't completely deflated, because he did spot a total of three lively saloons within a few short blocks. Where there's smoke, he thought, there's fire.

They found the three-story McAlester Arms Hotel standing between two humbler neighbors—a drugstore and a meat market. At the end of the street was an icehouse, the last stop before the prairie began once again. Across the street was a restaurant that advertised by means of a painted sign above its entrance: Home Cooking.

They entered the hotel and found themselves in a large lobby dotted with dusty palms in brass containers and overstuffed furniture that had seen better days. The lobby also contained a writing desk, with quill pens and an inkwell, and a small concession stand that sold newspapers and magazines.

"Good day." A clerk greeted Jessie and Ki as they arrived at the registration desk. "Welcome to McAlester."

They both signed the guest book he presented with just the hint of a flourish. He took it from them and, glancing at it, exclaimed, "Oh, I must say it is a great pleasure to have you with us, Miss Starbuck. Your name is very well known in this area. And, I hasten to add, much respected."

"Thank you," Jessie said.

"You both just arrived on the train, did you?"

"We did," Ki declared.

"I heard it was dreadfully late. Someone said there had been an accident."

"There was one of a sort," Ki agreed. "Also a robbery attempt."

"Really? Oh, dear me. What is the world coming to when people risk their lives traveling from one place to another. You both, I trust, escaped unscathed?"

"Neither one of us is the least bit scathed," Ki said solemnly, but he gave Jessie a surreptitious wink.

"Our room numbers?" Jessie prompted.

"Oh, you want separate rooms?"

"Yes."

"Certainly, Miss Starbuck. I had simply assumed—" The clerk, flustered, blushed. Then, recovering somewhat, he took down two keys from a rack on the wall behind him and presented them to Jessie and Ki. "Both rooms are on the second floor. Right up those stairs over there and turn right at the first landing. I trust you will enjoy your stay with us."

As Ki picked up their luggage and started for the stairs, Jessie asked the clerk if Mr. Luke Hodges was registered at the hotel.

"He most certainly is. He's in room number thirteen. Third floor front. But Mr. Hodges is not in at the moment, I'm afraid."

"Do you happen to know, by any chance, where he is at the moment?"

"I would say it is most likely—yes, highly likely—that he is out at his mine west of town."

"Thank you." Jessie left the desk and followed Ki up the stairs to their rooms on the second floor, which, she soon discovered, adjoined one another.

She unlocked her door and stood aside as Ki placed her luggage inside her room. Then she made arrangements with him to go out to the Hodges mine after they had unpacked and had time to freshen up.

"My goodness," Jessie exclaimed later that day as she drove through the countryside outside of McAlester in the rig she had rented at the livery. "There must be nearly a score more mines operating here now than there were when I was here last year."

She and Ki scanned the area, where open pit and underground mines seemed to cover almost the entire landscape. Men were hard at work in them. Mules hauled carts to open cars waiting on spur lines of the Katy railroad, where the coal was unloaded for its journey to market.

Coal dust drifted in the air. So did the echoes of the voices of the miners shouting to one another and the metallic ring of picks striking the sloping cliffs of coal in the pits. Shovels struck tin pails, and tin pails banged together as they were carried by miners to the waiting ore carts and dumped into them.

"There's nobody working over there," Ki observed with a nod of his head in the direction of a river shining in the sun as it wound past the entrance to an underground mine.

"That's one of Monty Carruthers's mines. It played out over a year ago. Knowing Monty, I'm sure he has established two more mines to make up for that one that's no longer of value."

"Who is Monty Carruthers?"

"I keep forgetting that you've never been here before. If you had, you'd surely know who Monty Carruthers is. He is, to say the least, a very successful businessman. He has a large mine operating in this area. He also has a recently hired field team to search for new deposits of coal. He is one of my fiercest competitors, and I use the word 'fiercest' advisedly."

Ki gave Jessie a questioning glance.

"Monty is a self-made man," she continued by way of explanation. "He's told me he had a long and difficult struggle to get where he is today, and I gather he let nothing stand in his way. Nothing and no one. He came of a large and dirt-poor family. I recall him saying he would do anything and everything he had to in order never to have to beg a thing of anyone ever again."

"You seem to know him very well."

"I do. One always should, I believe, get to know the nature and habits of anyone who could possibly pose a threat to one's own interest and well-being."

"Carruthers is that bad, huh?"

"He's no worse than most businessmen. Or businesswomen like me. We all fight tooth and nail to get ahead and to make money and so on. It's what we do. Some of us, like Monty Carruthers, do it very well."

Jessie fell silent as they approached a section of Katy spur line. She gripped the reins tightly and slowed her team. Even so, the carriage bounded and rattled as they crossed the rails and the ties supporting them.

37

Once on relatively smooth ground again, Jessie pointed. "That's where we're headed."

In the distance, Ki saw another open pit mine. Miners were perched on its steep slope like insects clinging to a nearly vertical wall as their picks tore into the blue-black coal of which the slope was composed. Down below them was a plank shack with a sign above its door which read simply, Hodges.

"That's Luke's mine," Jessie said. "He's probably there or somewhere nearby." She drove up to the shack and brought the carriage to a halt. A moment later, she was knocking on the door.

"Come in!" a male voice called out from inside.

She opened the door and, with Ki right behind her, went inside.

"Jessie!"

"Hello, Luke."

The man who had greeted her came out from behind his scarred wooden desk and threw his arms around Jessie. He hugged her, a broad smile on his face, and then held her out at arm's length and stared at her.

"It's good to see you again. It's more than good, it's wonderful!"

Luke Hodges was a tall man. He had a sturdy body that silently spoke of a life of hard labor and the strength that came from living such a life. But he moved with a catlike grace, and when he embraced Jessie, his movements were gentle, the actions of a man confident of his own strength, who needed no opportunity to display it.

He had a square face and a dimpled chin. His lips were full and suggested a sensual nature. His nose was aquiline and his brow broad above deeply set eyes that were as blue as a cloudless summer sky. His straight blond hair kept falling down across his forehead, giving him at times an almost boyish look.

Jessie, gazing into the depths of his warm eyes, said, "It's good to see you again, too, Luke. It's been too long a time since we last met."

"That was at the last annual meeting of Starbuck Enterprises' people last year," he said thoughtfully. "I remember it was spring, and you and I went for a drive. The daisies were in full bloom."

Ki glanced from Luke to Jessie and saw the light alive in her eyes as she continued to stare at Luke and he continued to hold her out in front of him as if he never intended to let her go again.

"They were lovely, the daisies," Jessie said softly.

"Yes. Yes, they were."

The pair continued to stare at one another in silence for a long moment before Jessie, seeming to awaken from a pleasant dream, said, "Luke, I'd like you to meet a very dear friend of mine. Ki, this is Luke Hodges, who leases this mine from Starbuck Enterprises."

"How do you do, Mr. Hodges," Ki said, offering his hand.

"Call me Luke," Hodges said as they shook hands. "I'm pleased to meet you, Ki. It's nice to know we have something in common."

"And what is that, Luke?" Ki inquired.

"Jessie's friendship."

Ki saw Hodges's eyes drift back to Jessie. There's more than friendship between them, he thought, or I miss my guess.

"Luke, why don't you tell us about the trouble you've been having here," Jessie suggested.

He released her and gestured to a pair of wooden chairs in front of his desk. "Sit down and I will." As they took the seats he had offered them, Hodges went around behind his desk and sat down. Folding his hands on the desk in front of him, he said, "The Choctaws want us out of here. Either that or they want us to pay them a higher royalty than has been the case in the past, if they're to allow us to continue mining on their land."

"The current royalty is one cent a ton, as I recall," Jessie commented. "What increase are they suggesting?"

"Ten cents a ton. And they're not suggesting; they're demanding."

"What is the general sentiment among the mine owners concerning their demand?" Jessie asked.

"They're against it. Men like Monty Carruthers flat out refuse to pay a penny more than they're already paying. Jessie, this operation of mine, it's not the richest coal deposit in the world. But it's no slouch either. I'm making money. But if I have to pay ten cents a ton to the Choctaw tribal treasury on top of the ordinary expenses connected with running the mine and paying my men—which includes the five cents per ton royalty I have to pay you—I'm liable to go under, and that's no fairy tale I'm telling you."

"You won't go under, Luke, I assure you. If worst comes to worst, Starbuck Enterprises will lend you the money you need to keep going."

"I appreciate your offer, Jessie, but it won't work. I mean to say that I'm in debt to you and to some of my suppliers as it is. Taking on more debt would not be the best or the smartest move I could make at this juncture."

"Is there anything else going on that I should know about, Luke?"

"Well, there's a chance we're going to be facing some labor trouble in what may turn out to be the near future. The miners want more pay and a shorter workday." Hodges unfolded his hands, leaned back in his chair, and sighed. "I tell you, Jessie, I'm getting belted from every angle it seems. I feel like a man with his back against the wall."

"I'll do everything I can to help, Luke."

"I know you will and I appreciate it, I truly do. I thought about things for a long time before I finally sent you that telegram. I'd been hoping I could handle matters on my own, but I finally decided I'd best let you know about what's going on here so that you could, as you said earlier, take any action you deem necessary to protect your own position in the coal fields."

"I'm glad you did contact me. I try to keep on top of things, but with worldwide interests—Well, it's not always possible to do so to the degree I would like. I have to depend on people like you to keep me appraised of current conditions."

"Maybe you could work out some sort of compromise with the Choctaws," Ki suggested, addressing both Jessie and Hodges.

"Maybe so," Hodges mused. "But their Principal Chief can be as stubborn as a mule with his mind made up."

"I intend to pay Chief Bryant a visit," Jessie said. "I intend to remind him when I do of the agreement he made with me when we first began mining coal here on Choctaw land."

Hodges laughed mirthlessly. "Agreement indeed. There's a movement afoot among the Indians to scrap all previous agreements and contracts of any kind made with the whites. There's a fellow leading that movement—his name's Daniel Marshal—who seems bound and determined to kick out all white miners, mine owners, and lessees like me and let the Choctaws themselves mine the coal and collect all the profits from its sale. Mine *Choctaw* coal as Marshal is pleased to call it."

"Why, that's preposterous!" Jessie exclaimed. "The Choctaws never did a damned thing about the coal deposits on their land before outfits like mine came along and made arrangements—with the full approval of and authorization from the duly appointed representatives of the Nation—to mine it ourselves and pay them for the privilege of doing so."

A smiling Hodges held up both hands, his palms facing Jessie, as if to ward off an attack. "Don't preach to me, Jessie. I'm already converted." Then, more seriously, he continued, "I'll tell you what I think's behind all this talk of Choctaw coal for the Choctaw people. Chief Bryant and Daniel Marshal and others who share their point of view want the baby and are willing to let us have the bathwater."

"The Choctaws never showed any interest in the coal fields before outfits like Starbuck Enterprises and others came along and began to turn them into a profitable resource," Jessie declared heatedly. "The coal just sat there and did no one any good, certainly not the Indians."

"Well, all that's changed now," Hodges said. "Now the Indians want to wring every dime that they can out of the operation of the mines, and to some of them, like Daniel Marshal, that means throwing the white mine operators and their employees out of their collective ears so that the Indians can feast on the whole hog once we're gone, not just the part of it that is represented by our royalty payments to the tribal treasury."

"What exactly do the Indians intend to do, Luke?" Jessie asked. "Try to take over the mines through their court system?"

"That's one option that Chief Bryant has talked about. But

that hothead, Daniel Marshal, he has other ideas. He's talking about taking back the mines by force."

"That's outrageous!" a clearly annoyed Jessie stated bluntly. "What about the thousands of dollars I and others like me—Monty Carruthers, for example—have invested in our mining operations? Does this—What did you say that man's name was?"

"Daniel Marshal."

"What does Daniel Marshal propose to do about that?"

"Quite frankly, Jessie," Hodges said solemnly, "I don't think Mr. Marshal gives two hoots in a holler about our investment in the mines. That, he would probably say, is our problem."

"Well, I intend to make it his problem."

Ki's eyebrows arched in mild surprise. "You do? How?"

"By pointing out to him that what he appears to be advocating—"

"There's no 'appears' about it, Jessie," Hodges interrupted. "He is very definitely and openly advocating the seizure of the mines and all their assets because he and others like him believe they are rightfully the property of Choctaw Nation and that the only people who should benefit from them are the individual citizens of Choctaw Nation. And that, by the way, is where still another source of conflict arises."

"I don't think you need another one," Ki said mildly.

"Nevertheless we've got one," Hodges declared.

"What is it you're getting at, Luke?" Jessie asked, leaning forward in her chair.

"Daniel Marshal and Chief Joseph Bryant are at loggerheads over the question of who should get the money from the mines if they are taken over by the Indians or if there is merely an increase in the royalty rates paid the Nation by owners such as yourself, who have leased the operation of their holdings to men like me. Marshal insists the monies should be shared directly by individual citizens of Choctaw Nation. Chief Bryant, on the other hand, wants the money to go directly into the tribal treasury, to be used as he sees fit. To improve the Choctaw school system, for example."

Jessie sat back in her chair. "This is a complex issue, I'm beginning to realize. I just hope that reason and common sense will prevail in the end."

"Whose reason and common sense?" Ki asked innocently. "Yours or the Indians'?"

"We should be able to reach a suitable compromise," Jessie stated. "We can sit down together and discuss the matter, and with each of us willing to compromise on certain points, we should end up with a satisfactory resolution of the problems."

"It's worth a try," Ki said.

"Let's go back to town now," Jessie suggested. "I want to have a talk with Chief Bryant as soon as possible, and he has an office in McAlester."

"You'll have to wait, Jessie," Hodges said. "Bryant is out of town on tribal business. He's not expected back before tomorrow."

"Well then maybe I could—"

"Jessie, it's getting rather late in the day to conduct business," Ki pointed out. "Why not rest a bit and tackle these problems tomorrow when you can get a fresh start?"

"I think Ki's right," Hodges said. "You just got into town today, am I right?"

Jessie nodded.

"A little rest and relaxation might be in order for the rest of the day and tonight. And speaking of such, I wonder if you two would consider having dinner with me this evening."

Jessie glanced at Ki. "That's fine with me. Ki?"

"I have other plans," he lied, deciding that Hodges would much prefer to have dinner alone with Jessie. "I hope you two will excuse me."

"Why, of course," Hodges said quickly, to Ki's mild chagrin.

"What time this evening, Luke?" Jessie asked, making no effort to try to persuade Ki to change his mind about joining them.

"I'm staying at the McAlester Arms—"

"I know," Jessie said. "I checked." She blushed when Hodges gave her a penetrating glance.

"You're registered there as well?"

"Yes."

"Good. Suppose then I call for you at eight."

"Fine. I'll be waiting."

• • •

Jessie was dabbing rose water on her neck and behind her ears with the glass stopper of the scent's bottle when the knock sounded on her hotel room door at exactly eight o'clock that evening. She quickly stoppered the bottle, put it down, fluffed her hair in front of the mirror above the dresser, adjusted her skirt, and then opened the door, a smile on her face.

"Right on time as usual," she said to Luke Hodges, who was standing, Stetson in both hands, in the hall.

"You remembered."

"That you are always on time for appointments? Yes, I did. I remembered one or two other things, mostly pleasant, about you as well."

"Just *mostly* pleasant?" Hodges inquired, arching an eyebrow at Jessie as she admitted him to her room.

"I was remembering your temper, which you displayed in my presence on one or two occasions."

"I do have a short fuse, I must admit. I have absolutely no patience with fools or knaves. I do not suffer them readily. But you, Jessie, are neither a fool nor a knave, so I can practically guarantee that you will see no display of the famed—the infamous—Hodges temper tonight. Although I cannot make the same guarantee for the duration of your stay in McAlester, since it may well be that you shall see me in head-to-head confrontation with one or more fools or knaves."

"Shall we go?"

Hodges picked up the shawl that was draped over the back of a chair and placed it around Jessie's shoulders. "What else do you remember about me—about us?"

"Everything."

Hodges bent his head and pressed his lips to the base of Jessie's throat.

She caught her breath as she bent her head backward to receive the caress of his hot lips. When his arms went around her and he drew her close to him, she broke from his embrace.

"Is something wrong?" he asked, perplexed. "Has something changed between us, Jessie?"

"No, it's not that. It's just that I'm hungry and you did promise me a meal, as I recall."

"I'm hungry, too," he said huskily, reaching for her again.

44

She managed to evade him. "Later," she whispered.

"Is that a promise?"

"Most definitely."

He offered her his arm and she took it, allowing him to escort her out of the room and then out of the hotel. On the way to the restaurant Hodges had mentioned to her earlier, they made small talk about nothing in particular—the weather, the brilliance of the stars in the night sky above them, the hordes of fireflies flitting through the darkness.

Once in the restaurant, Hodges waved away the menus the waiter brought to their table and said, "Trust me, Jessie, to order for you." When she nodded, he ordered broiled bear meat, a garden salad, and baked potatoes with sour cream.

"The fare here will never compete with Delmonico's in New York or even with the best that St. Louis restaurants have to offer, but it's good and the portions are plentiful."

Jessie looked around the large room, which was decorated with potted plants and oil paintings of pastoral scenes. The patrons, she nodded, were mostly sedate Choctaw men and women who seemed not to belong in the midst of the volatile environment Hodges had described to her earlier in the day. There was also a sprinkling of hard-bitten men who looked as if they had scrubbed themselves thoroughly for their evening out, but who could not nevertheless hide all the nearly indelible marks of the mines that they bore—faint traces of coal dust ingrained in the leathery folds of their skin and thick calluses on their hands.

"This is the first time in a long time." Hodges commented, "that I've had a chance to mix business with pleasure."

"I hope you're not going to spoil our evening together with talk of business, Luke."

"I'm not, I promise you. I merely meant that the fact of us being together is, essentially, a wedding of business and pleasure since the two of us are linked on both levels."

"I still remember that night we spent together after the annual meeting."

"We had to act like conspirators about to pull off some sort of nefarious plot, so no one would know what we were up to. I refer to the way we had to go our separate ways as if we had no interest in bidding one another so much as the time of day, only to wend our secretive ways to the local hotel and the previously rented room with the big brass bed."

"No one ever suspected us of—what should we call it? Collusion?"

"A terrible name for a delightful encounter."

"What about merger?"

"That does seem to define it, but I have never before heard of lovemaking between a man and a woman called a merger."

The waiter arrived with their meals, and Jessie, suppressing a giggle, began at once to eat.

Hodges, his fork poised above his split and steaming baked potato, watched her take dainty bites of her bear steak. "Jessie, I can't tell you how wonderful it is to be with you again like this."

She smiled but said nothing as she continued to eat.

Later, over coffee, she said, "I think it's time we were on our way."

"Whooppeee!" said Hodges with exaggerated glee.

Once back in Jessie's hotel room, he repeated the word, more softly but still with feeling as he took Jessie in his arms and kissed her passionately.

She eagerly returned his kiss, and soon their lips parted and Hodges's tongue was exploring her mouth. She teased it with her own, causing him to moan and hold her even more tightly. Her hands roamed up and down his strong, broad back as he cupped her buttocks and pressed her pelvis against his own, which was twisting and grinding into hers.

His actions aroused Jessie, and she groaned now as he had done earlier. Her own pelvis matched the distinctly erotic rhythm of his as their lips parted and they stood there for a moment, both of them breathing heavily, both of them thoroughly aroused.

Then, as Hodges buried his face in her neck and nuzzled it, she began to unbutton his coat. Then his shirt. Then she unbuckled his belt and undid the buttons of his fly.

"Oh, Jessie," he groaned and hurriedly began to remove his clothes, flinging them toward a nearby chair and not noticing or caring when some of the garments missed their intended target and fell on the floor.

Minutes later, they were both nude and lying side by side

46

on the room's soft bed. Hodges ran a finger around Jessie's breasts and then bent his head and briefly sucked each of them, causing her nipples to harden. Her hand reached out and gripped his stone-stiff shaft. Gently, she caressed its above-average length and bulk. She squeezed it several times and then began to stroke it in a swift up-and-down movement.

He reached down and removed her hand. "I'm so close to coming," he said. "I don't want to do it that way." He pressed her down on her back on the bed and then straddled her. He stared down at her for a moment as she gazed up at him and her tongue flicked out to moisten her lush lips.

"Among the things I remembered about our last encounter," she murmured, "was what you like best." She pursed her lips, raised a finger to touch them and then transferred an airy kiss to the head of his massive manhood, which was throbbing as it seemed to paw the air above her bare body.

He eased his body up alongside her own until his knees were next to her breasts. He reached behind her and positioned the bed's two pillows so that they supported her head. Then, taking his erection in his right hand, he brought it into contact with her still slightly parted lips.

She opened her mouth and closed her eyes as he slowly eased his shaft between her lips and then all the way into her welcoming mouth. He moaned as he felt her tongue begin to lave him. He placed the palms of his hands on the wall behind the bed and began to move his hips in a slow, sensuous rhythm, his head lowered to watch his cock slide out from between Jessie's lips and then slide back down into her throat as she continued sucking on it and her tongue continued to send tremors of delight throughout his body.

He continued thrusting and she continued sucking, her hands gripping his bare buttocks and at times forcing him all the way into her mouth. She held him there as her tongue worked its wonders on his stiff member, until he thought he could stand no more of the exquisite pleasure she was giving him with the slick movements of her tongue and the pressure of her lovely lips on him.

"Soon," he managed to mutter through partially clenched teeth. "Soon, honey."

Jessie increased her efforts, gripping his buttocks firmly in both hands, her eyes still closed as she seemed to be trying to suck his very essence out of his shaft. He exploded a moment later, the world blasting away from him for a thrilling number of minutes as surge after surge of his seed shot from his cock and into Jessie's still-sucking mouth.

She made soft sounds and her Adam's apple worked feverishly as she swallowed all he had to give. Then, reluctantly, she relaxed her hold on him and he withdrew from her mouth. A wave of temporary weakness washed over him as he slumped back down on the bed beside her. "Wonderful," he managed to whisper. "You were."

"It was just like old times, wasn't it?" she whispered in his ear.

"Better."

She sighed and stretched, her left hand coming to rest on his slowly softening shaft. "It's tuckered," she whispered, smiling at him.

"Not that tuckered," he insisted as he rolled over on top of her, and then, as stiffness swiftly returned to his eager member, he entered her and began to pound down upon her. She cried out within seconds of his eager entry, to signal the first of what proved to be multiple climaxes.

★

Chapter 4

"What in the world is making that racket?" Jessie exclaimed next morning as she and Ki left the restaurant where they had breakfasted, the same restaurant where she had dined the night before with Luke Hodges.

The sound of clanging metal reverberated throughout the street. People scurried toward its source, which neither Jessie nor Ki could see from where they stood outside the restaurant.

"A fire?" Ki speculated.

But he quickly rejected that idea when no fire apparatus appeared and no sign of flames could be seen in the direction from which the almost ear-splitting sound was coming.

"Let's go and see what it is," Jessie suggested.

"I thought we were on our way to pay a visit to Monty Carruthers," Ki pointed out.

"We will visit Monty. But first—"

"Let's satisfy your woman's curiosity?"

"I suppose you couldn't care less what all that racket is about."

"I admit I am mildly curious."

"Mildly!" Jessie exclaimed and gave him a skeptical glance before hurrying down the street with the other people who were heading in the same direction.

Ki had to run to keep up with her.

As they joined the throng that had gathered at the intersection where the metallic banging was the loudest, Jessie, with Ki following, shouldered her way to the front of the crowd.

As the clanging continued, she resisted the defensive impulse to clap her hands over her ears to block out the annoying sound, which she and Ki were now able to see was being made by a Choctaw Indian banging a long metal spoon on the bottom of a tin washtub.

Another Choctaw, a handsome young man in his twenties, joined the man with the washtub and climbed up on a soapbox he had placed on the ground next to his colleague. As he held up his hands, his colleague stopped banging the washtub and the crowd quieted.

"Ladies and gentlemen, for those of you who don't know me," he began, "my name is Daniel Marshal and I'm a full-fledged and full-blooded citizen of Choctaw Nation, as many of you also are. I want to talk to you today about the way our beloved republic is being exploited by the men who are digging precious coal out of our earth and selling it for huge profits while paying us a pittance—a *pittance*, I say, ladies and gentlemen—for that privilege."

"Hear, hear!" the washtub banger shouted, punctuating his call with a single teeth-jarring bang on his tin tub.

"You all know," Marshal continued, "that white men have come in here without the permission of the ordinary citizens of our republic and have, since their arrival, proceeded to steal our coal to satisfy their lust for money and still more money."

"We pay you for that right!" Jessie shouted, unable to restrain herself in the face of Marshal's wild rhetoric. "And not a pittance as you claim but a decent and fair sum of money. One that has been agreed upon by your own Principal Chief, the honorable Joseph Bryant."

"Who, fair lady, might you be?" Marshal called out, his black eyes boring into Jessie's own.

"My name is Jessica Starbuck and I—"

"There, ladies and gentlemen," Marshal cried, pointing an indicting finger at Jessie, "stands one of the exploiters of Choctaw Nation and its valuable resources. Have you heard the infamous name before? Jessica Starbuck is one of the prime destroyers of our land. One of the thieves who are taking from us the resources that belong to all the citizens of Choctaw Nation."

"How dare you, Mr. Marshal!" Jessie shouted, her voice harsh. "I am not a thief, nor am I a destroyer of your land. I own a mine that I lease to a responsible man who mines coal, yes, but he shares the money he earns by so doing by making previously agreed upon contributions to your tribal treasury."

"Take it easy, Jessie," Ki cautioned. "If you keep arguing with him the way you are, you're liable to start a riot right here in the middle of the street."

Jessie ignored her friend's cautionary words. "I defy you to contradict me, Mr. Marshal," she cried, shaking a fist at him.

"One cent a ton, ladies and gentlemen," Marshal bellowed, turning from side to side, his eyes sweeping the rapt crowd before him. "A most munificent contribution to the tribal treasury, wouldn't you say?" He didn't wait for an answer. "A crime is what I call it, certainly not largesse. No, not largesse by any manner of means. Mine owners like Miss Starbuck there—*white* mine owners—together with the highway robbers associated with the Missouri, Kansas, and Texas Railroad, are the ones who are stealing us all blind."

Jessie tried to say something, but Marshal's resonant voice effectively drowned her out.

"I say let us petition the Choctaw Legislature to rescind the contracts that have been made with the likes of Miss Starbuck. Declare them all null and void *now*!"

A cheer went up from the crowd.

Clearly encouraged, Marshal continued, "The coal that lies within the boundaries of our republic is *our* coal. If it is to be mined and sold for profit, let us be the ones to mine it and reap the profits it brings for the benefit of the republic and all of its citizens."

"You speak the truth, Danny," a man in the crowd called out. "Let's take back what is rightfully ours in the first place!"

"Wait a minute!" Jessie called out. "What is this 'take back' talk? I always thought the Choctaws were a law-abiding people. A people who honored contracts honorably agreed upon. Contracts such as the one I have with your people."

"Lies and devilish deceit!" shouted a man standing not far from Jessie. "People like you come here and speak sly words that confuse us. So we give away our coal to you, not knowing what it is we do."

Jessie, furious at the accusation, which she knew to be totally false, could barely speak for a moment. She found her voice, however, when she noticed the smug expression on the face of Daniel Marshal as he stood with his arms folded on top of his soapbox and waited for her next move.

"You did not give away your coal to us," she insisted. "We pay you for it."

"The pittance I mentioned a moment ago," Marshal interjected. "One pitiful cent a ton. Bear in mind, ladies and gentlemen, when you consider that figure, that coal is currently selling on the open market at eleven dollars a ton. Eleven dollars, I say. Where, then, is the fairness or the justice in a deal like that?"

"Raise the royalty rate!" a woman shouted, brandishing the umbrella she was using to ward off the morning's already hot sun.

"Double it!" someone else cried. "We deserve at least two cents a ton for our coal."

"Two cents a ton," Marshal repeated, sadly shaking his head. "Ladies and gentlemen, I beg you not to think in such paltry—such pygmy—terms. We Choctaws, ladies and gentlemen, are the giants in this situation. We are the ones who own the coal in question. We should not be considering whether to charge a royalty of two or ten or twenty cents a ton for that coal. The royalty rate, I submit to you, is not the issue here. Ownership is the issue. And it is an issue easily decided by fair-minded people. *We* own the coal!"

"So what do we do about the problem, Daniel?" a man asked.

"I say we all attend the next session of the Choctaw Legislature when it convenes and—"

"Those lousy politicians won't be in session for nigh on to

another week, Daniel," the same man pointed out, contempt in his tone. "Besides which, what do we need them for? We can march on the coal fields and take them back by force if necessary."

The crowd loudly cheered the man's angry words.

Marshal, frowning, surveyed the crowd, obviously trying to judge its sentiment and the strength of that sentiment. "Is that what you want?" he called out.

"You bet it is," someone replied to more cheers.

Marshal hesitated a moment and then declared, "March we will, ladies and gentlemen. We will gather together our little army and we will march until victory is ours!"

This time the rousing cheers were accompanied by the sound Marshal's colleague made as he banged his metal spoon on his tin washbasin.

"When, Danny?"

Marshal looked down at the man who had asked the question, standing in the middle of the crowd. "When? When will we march? Why, today, that's when. This very afternoon. Men, go and tell your friends and relatives about our plan. Then we will all meet right back here at two o'clock this afternoon and march to the mines with our banners and our heads held high."

Jessie stood gnawing her lower lip as the excited crowd began to disperse. She kept her eyes on Marshal, who was talking to his colleague, and then, making up her mind, she strode up to him.

Ki followed her. He arrived at her side just in time to hear her say, "Mr. Marshal, I want a word with you."

"I'll see you this afternoon, Russ," Marshal said to the man with the washbasin and spoon. Then, turning to Jessie, he said, "Speak your piece, Miss Starbuck. I am a busy man. I have plans to make and many things to do between now and two o'clock. What is it you want to say to me?"

Jessie hardly knew where to begin. "What you're doing—it's reprehensible. Not to mention irresponsible. Do you really intend to lead an attack on the miners in the coal fields?"

"You heard the people, Miss Starbuck," Marshal answered. "That's what they want."

"What I heard," Ki said, "was a mob speaking with a mob's

mind. Never a pretty sound, Mr. Marshal."

"Who, sir, are you?"

"This man is a friend of mine," Jessie said. "His name is Ki."

"Well, I can't say, Miss Starbuck, that any friend of yours is a friend of mine, now can I, considering that you and I aren't friends to begin with. Enemies, would be more like it."

"We don't have to be enemies, Mr. Marshal. We could sit down and discuss the matter of the operation of the coal mines along with other interested parties."

"What other interested parties, Miss Starbuck?"

"The Choctaw Council, for one example. Chief Joseph Bryant, for another. Representatives of the Choctaw Legislature, who had a hand, a very strong one, in negotiating the original arrangement under which mine owners such as myself operate our businesses."

"I suppose you would also want to include Leonard Fanshaw of the Katy railroad, who is making money hand over fist by shipping coal hither and yon at a handsome profit to the line. And we mustn't forget the men who have leased the mines from their owners such as yourself."

"Yes, they should be included in any discussions we have, since they have a strong stake in the outcome of such discussions and would want to make their point of view on the matter known."

"Miss Starbuck, let me tell you something that might help to simplify things. I don't give a good goddam about any lessees or about the operators of the Katy railroad or the Choctaw Council either for that matter. All I care about—"

"All you care about, Mr. Marshal," Jessie interrupted, "is promoting your own narrow point of view to the exclusion of everybody else's!"

"You're right! That's true. And I'll tell you something else. My point of view—which you have just heard expressed here today—is shared by many other people. People who are willing to fight—to lay their lives on the line if that should become necessary—to get what they want and damn well deserve."

"Then you're not willing to sit down and talk—"

"When the Choctaw people once again have possession of what is and always has been rightfully theirs—maybe then I'll

54

think about sitting down and talking with you and others like you, Miss Starbuck. But not one minute before that time."

"You know, I suppose, that I lease a mine I own to Mr. Luke Hodges," Jessie said icily.

"I know that."

"Well, there's something else you should know. If you try to make trouble today or at any other time for Mr. Hodges—which means, in the final analysis, for me—you will have to contend with me and the efforts I will make to stop you dead in your dangerous tracks, Mr. Marshal."

"A very pretty speech. Very pretty indeed. But you're wasting your breath and your time preaching to me, Miss Starbuck."

"Be that as it may, Mr. Marshal, I've said what I wanted to say."

As Jessie turned and stalked away, Ki said, "Mr. Marshal, since coming to this country from Japan I've heard a lot of interesting American expressions. There's one I think maybe I ought to mention to you at this juncture. It's this: 'A word to the wise is sufficient.' "

Before Marshal could say anything more, Ki turned and went after Jessie.

"He's insufferable," Jessie said when Ki had joined her and they made their way toward the office of the mine owner Monty Carruthers.

"He's also dangerous, in my opinion," Ki commented as they turned a corner. "You told him you intended to do everything within your power to stop him and what he's planning. I'm wondering what you had in mind."

Jessie hesitated a moment and then said, "I don't know what to do to tell you the truth."

"You were bluffing then."

This time Jessie's answer came quickly, without any hesitation. "No, not really. To say that I don't know exactly what to do is not to say that I was bluffing back there. I'll think of something."

When they arrived at Carruthers's office, they found the door open and went inside, where a young woman with luxuriant coils of russet hair piled high on her head smiled and asked if she could help them.

"My name is Jessica Starbuck," Jessie began. "I'm here to

see Mr. Carruthers. I apologize for not having an appointment, but I haven't had time to make one."

"I'll see if Mr. Carruthers is able to see you now, Miss Starbuck. Please have a seat. It'll only be a moment."

When the woman returned, Jessie and Ki were still standing. "You may go right in," she told them.

"Jessie, my dear!" Carruthers exclaimed as they entered his office. He clasped Jessie's hands in both of his large ones and led her to a chair. "Do sit down. Let me look at you. You look absolutely ravishing, my dear. Exactly as I remember you from our last meeting. Tell me something. How do you manage to stay so ageless?"

"It's a secret, but I'll reveal it to you. I thrive on a diet of flattery from such gentlemen as yourself, Monty."

Carruthers released her hands. He turned to Ki and held out his hand. "I don't believe I've had the pleasure, sir."

"My name's Ki. I'm a friend of Jessie's."

"Welcome to McAlester, Ki," Carruthers said as they shook hands. Turning his attention back to Jessie, he asked, "What brings you to town, my dear?"

"I received a telegram from Luke Hodges," Jessie began.

"He's the young man who leases your coal mine from you, am I correct?"

"Yes, you are. Luke alerted me to the fact that there are a number of problems connected with the mining operations in the area, so Ki and I came up here on the train to see for ourselves what's going on."

Carruthers threw his hands up into the air, rounded his desk, and sat down in a swivel chair behind it. "It's the Indians," he declared. "They're as greedy as King Croesus. They're threatening to run us out of the territory, did you know?" Without waiting for an answer from Jessie, Carruthers continued, "Well, this is one man that is not being run out of town on a rail, I can assure you."

"I'm glad to hear of your resolve to fight back, Monty," Jessie said. "Ki and I just ran into Daniel Marshal, who was addressing a crowd on a street corner not far from here." Jessie proceeded to explain the substance of Marshal's speech to the crowd he had gathered.

"A rabble-rouser of the first order," Carruthers commented

derisively when she had concluded her account. "Marshal is a man with an out-of-control social conscience. He believes that the mines and the coal in them should simply be handed over by us to the citizens of Choctaw Nation without regard to the fact that we have signed agreements permitting us to mine that coal."

"Marshal has threatened to march, he and any mob he can muster to his side, on the mines," Jessie said. "If he does, there is no telling what may happen. There may even be bloodshed, if I read that firebrand correctly."

"He's not the only troublemaker we have to concern ourselves with," Carruthers declared, a gloomy expression on his face. "There's also Caleb Pace."

"Who is he?" Ki inquired.

"He's a miner who works for me. He has been busy making mischief right along with Daniel Marshal, albeit of a quite different kind.

"Caleb Pace, it seems, is urging the miners to go on strike to force us to pay higher wages and to improve what he is pleased to call 'unsafe working conditions.' He had been complaining of insufficient ventilation in the underground mines, which he claims is a clear and present danger to the limbs and lives of the miners because of the volatile gases which tend to accumulate in coal mines."

"Well, I must say," Jessie commented thoughtfully, "Pace has a valid point there. Only last year Luke Hodges's mine had a minor explosion. As a result, he sank nearly a dozen additional air shafts into the tunnels to prevent a reoccurrence of such a thing."

"Such shafts cost money," Carruthers complained, folding his hands across his paunchy midriff. "They reduce our net profit."

Jessie, somewhat surprised at the man's reaction to the problem they were discussing, chose to remain silent, although she found her colleague's position disturbing. What good was a mine after a gas explosion had destroyed it and many, if not all, of the men working in it? She was as cost-conscious as anyone else in business, but she was also keenly aware that one could carry cost-cutting and cost-reductions to a point of diminishing—or no—returns.

Carruthers interrupted her thoughts with "If Caleb Pace thinks he's going to break me, he's as wrong as red rain. If he and the men backing him decide to go out on strike, well, they'll rue the day they did, I guarantee you."

"But if that happens, if they do strike," Jessie said, wondering what Carruthers was getting at, "you'll lose money and lose it fast, Monty. If Pace should shut down your mine, you'll earn nothing during the time the strike lasts. Maybe it would be better if you—all of us—discussed the issues with Pace to see if we can come to some sort of reasonable settlement."

"That sounds sensible to me," Ki offered.

"I have to disagree with both of you," Carruthers blustered, his face beginning to flush. "What neither of you seems to understand is one simple fact. That fact is this. If we give an inch to these miners who are trying to bleed us dry, they'll take a yard. Soon even that yard will not be enough to satisfy them. They will want another yard and then still another. In time, they could bankrupt us."

"What alternative are you considering, Mr. Carruthers?" Ki asked. "If there is a strike, what counter-action do you intend to take?"

Carruthers smiled. "For every man who is willing to strike my mine, there are two—nay, as many as ten—who will willingly work for the wages I now pay and under the conditions that presently exist in my mine."

"You're considering hiring strike breakers in the event of a strike action," Jessie said.

"I have already put out the word through contacts I have in the area that if my workers go on strike I will immediately be in the market to hire men to replace them."

"Monty, I understand your position and I cannot fault you for trying to continue operating in the face of labor strife," Jessie said. "But let me ask you to consider this, if I may."

Carruthers frowned at Jessie as he waited for her to continue.

"The men, if they indeed do go on strike at your mine, aren't likely to take passively the hiring of other men to replace them. After all, their livelihoods will be at stake and I think that desperate men will take desperate actions to protect their source of income—"

"If they want to protect their source of income," Carruthers angrily interrupted, "let them remain on the job where they belong."

Unperturbed by the interruption, Jessie continued, "The striking miners would, I am sure, do battle with the men you bring in to replace them. It has happened elsewhere in the country. It's a situation where, in the end, almost no one wins. And a lot lose. Sometimes, they lose their lives. I have to repeat that I think we should talk to Caleb Pace and see what we can work out together before there is outright labor warfare in the coal fields."

"Jessie," Carruthers said sadly, "you know I have always admired your business acumen. But I must now say something I have never said before, although I have often thought it. Women don't belong in business. Oh, they do reasonably well and, in your case, exceptionally well, when things are running smoothly. But when trouble rears its ugly head, they wilt in the face of it. You suggest talking to Caleb Pace. Well, I say to you in all sincerity, talk is not what will work with Pace. Raw force will. You talk to him if you so choose. I'll hire men to talk to *my* miners through the barrels of guns if they make trouble for me."

Ki, glancing at Jessie, could see that she was fuming inwardly. He waited for the explosion.

It never came. Instead, Jessie said in a tone of sweet reasonableness, "I hope we won't have to face labor trouble, Monty. If we do, you will have to handle it in your way and I in mine."

Carruthers harrumphed. "You know, setting aside the potential problem with the miners and their discontent that has been so carefully cultivated by Caleb Pace, the Indians, in my opinion, are the greater problem facing us. On the one hand you have Daniel Marshal, who wants to take over the mines and distribute their earnings on an equal basis to all the citizens of Choctaw Nation, and on the other hand you have Chief Bryant, who also wants the money from the mines— either through Indian ownership or through increased royalty payments—but he wants the money so derived to go into the tribal treasury to be dispersed not to individual citizens but for things like schools, agricultural subsidies, and the like. The two men are at loggerheads on the issue. Which, it now occurs

59

to me even as I speak, might be good for our side."

"I don't understand, Monty."

"If the Indians are divided on tactical details—and they most definitely are at the moment—then perhaps we can exploit that division to our own advantage."

"How?" Ki prompted.

"I don't know," Carruthers said. "But there may be something there. I shall have to think about it."

"In the meantime," Jessie said, "we have Daniel Marshal to worry about. What do you plan to do to protect your mine, Monty, from any detrimental actions he and those who support him might take against it?"

"I intend to hire men, arm them, and post them around my mine to defend it against Marshal and his ragtag army of supporters."

"You really think that's the best way of dealing with the problem?" Jessie inquired.

"You heard him speak earlier this morning, you told me. Did you find a way to persuade him to back off?"

Jessie had to admit to herself that Carruthers was right; she had not been able to dissuade Marshal from his planned course of action.

"I take your silence, Jessie, for an admission that you failed to do so. I would therefore advise you to do what I am going to do. Hire men to defend your mine. I'm sure Luke Hodges will be willing to fight for what is his through his lease arrangement with you. Arm your miners if they are willing to fight. Then we shall see what Mr. Marshal does in the face of such determined opposition to his planned course of action."

"Monty, it's been good seeing you again," Jessie said, rising. "I've got to go out to the mine Luke Hodges operates and alert him to the possibility of trouble with Daniel Marshal and his men."

Carruthers and Ki also rose. Carruthers came out from behind his desk and shook hands with Ki and then with Jessie, to whom he said, "I'm sorry we don't see eye-to-eye about how to handle the problems facing us, but I hope that doesn't mean we're not still good friends."

"Of course it doesn't, Monty. Old friends can disagree without becoming enemies."

"I'm glad to hear that you feel that way, Jessie. We go back a long ways, you and I." Carruthers smiled. "I have a feeling that in time you'll come around to seeing things my way on this. Meanwhile, I intend to continue prospecting for new coal deposits. There is a fortune to be made here, Jessie, and I intend to make it. My researchers tell me they have preliminary indications that there may be rich deposits of coal just a few miles south of McAlester. If that proves to be true, and I fervently pray that it does, then I intend to mine those deposits, and no man is going to stop me from doing so. I've already had a talk with Leonard Fanshaw—I believe you know Leonard, don't you, Jessie?"

"Yes, I know him."

"Well, I've talked to Leonard and made tentative arrangements to have him run a spur line from his Katy railroad out to the new coal fields—if they pan out—so that we can more readily ship the coal to market. Oh, there are good times ahead for us, Jessie. There are, that is, if we can keep the troublemakers and the Indians in their respective places."

Later, as they made their way toward the center of town, Jessie said to Ki, "I don't like the way Monty Carruthers is thinking. He's too combative for my taste. Not that I'm not a fighter. I am, as you know. But there are many different ways of fighting to gain one's objective and not all of them involve violence."

"You may be right, but—"

When Ki fell silent, Jessie turned to him and asked, "But?"

"But I'm thinking of another American saying that I think is pithy and to the present point perhaps. 'Fight fire with fire.' "

"It may come to that in time," Jessie grudgingly admitted. "I just hope it doesn't."

"Are we heading out to the Hodges mine?"

"I had planned to, but now I have another idea. I think I ought to go and have a chat with Chief Bryant. He has a home just outside of town."

"You're going to try to convince the chief to see things your way?"

"Yes. But there is a more immediate matter I want to talk to him about. I want to try to persuade him to help stop Daniel

61

Marshal from causing any trouble out at the Hodges mine."

"How in the world do you expect to accomplish that? Both Daniel Marshal and Chief Bryant are Choctaws. Bryant isn't liable to side with you against one of his own people who is fighting you and the other mine owners."

"We'll see about that," Jessie said cryptically and added, "I wonder if you would do me a favor."

"Sure I would. Name it and it's as good as done."

"I'd appreciate it if you'd go out to the mine and warn Luke about what Daniel Marshal is planning. Tell him that Marshal just might try to make trouble at our mine instead of one of the others, especially in light of the fact that I challenged him at that street-corner rally he held this morning. I have a strong feeling he'd like to get even with me for that, and the best way to do that would be to make trouble at the Hodges mine."

"I'll do it," Ki assured her.

"Good. Thank you. I'll see you later. Either at the mine or back at the hotel."

"I'm surprised you came to me, Miss Starbuck," said Chief Joseph Bryant as he sat across from Jessie in the main room of his house. "Antagonism, unfortunately, rather than a spirit of cooperation exists between you and me."

Bryant was a stern-visaged man in his late forties. His skin was weathered and had the quality of burnt bark. His eyes were black as India ink beneath an overhanging brow and so were his hair and shaggy eyebrows. There was about him an aura of barely suppressed anger.

"There need not be antagonism between us, Chief," Jessie said. "I came here in the hope that we could work together to solve the problem I just told you about in a way that is satisfactory to both of us."

"You mine owners talk a good tale," Bryant declared, steepling his fingers and glowering at Jessie. "But in the end, and always, you act to protect your own self-interest, not the best interests of my people."

"It may have been that way in the past," Jessie was forced to admit. "But it needn't continue to be. And I must add that when you and I worked out our agreement some time ago concerning Starbuck Enterprises' right to mine coal here, I was more than willing to grant generous terms to you and did so even though it upset many of the other mine owners in the area with whom you were then also negotiating."

"Granted, Miss Starbuck."

Encouraged, Jessie continued, "You were, as I recall, Chief, delighted to sign that agreement with me at the time. You were pleased that the coal, which had before that point lain unmined and therefore worthless, would be mined and royalties would flow into the tribal treasury as they have done. We are talking, let me remind you, of many thousands of dollars a year in revenues that have been accruing to Choctaw Nation as a result of the development of the coal fields. I believe, if memory serves me correctly, that you reaped a bonanza of over six hundred thousand dollars last year alone, and with recently increased production on the part of most mine owners, you stand to earn far more than that sum this year."

"I grant that also, Miss Starbuck. But let me remind you that the monies of which you speak are nowhere near the monies people like yourself take from the mines—and out of Choctaw Nation—to spend elsewhere."

"You're saying then that you want all the money."

"I am not saying that. Please don't put words in my mouth, Miss Starbuck. I am simply suggesting that the citizens of Choctaw Nation are not receiving their fair share of the proceeds of the mines."

"Chief, that is a subject that we can discuss at another time. Right now, as I explained to you earlier, there is a more pressing matter that must be attended to. It is that matter which brought me here today."

"What makes you think I would act on your behalf against Daniel Marshal, a Choctaw Indian like myself?"

"Chief, Mr. Marshal does not see the matter of the mines and the revenue they generate in quite the same way that you do. Or so I have been given to understand. Mr. Marshal wants to take over the mines. You want to increase the royalty payments the mine owners pay the republic. Mr. Marshal wants to distribute the income from the mines, once they are taken over by your people, to individual citizens. You want the monies to be deposited into the tribal treasury and used for the greater good of the Nation as a whole. I thought you might be willing to see to it that Mr. Marshal does not achieve his goal of taking over the mines by force. If you were to do that, you really should not think of it as helping me and the other mine owners. You would be defeating a rival, not helping us."

The faintest trace of a smile ghosted across the chief's stern features. "You are a clever woman, Miss Starbuck. You know how to manipulate men."

"Have I spoken falsely, Chief?"

A pause and then a curt shake of the head. "I will do as you asked, Miss Starbuck."

"Thank you, Chief," Jessie said as she got to her feet and held out her hand.

The chief remained seated. He ignored her outstretched hand. "We must talk another time, Miss Starbuck," he said, staring intently up at her. "The trouble between us is far from over. It is most certainly not settled."

"I am glad to hear you say that we will talk and not fight, Chief," Jessie said as she withdrew her hand.

"I did not quite say that. I said we will talk. I did not say that we will not someday fight if fighting becomes the way to gain what is good for the Choctaw people."

Jessie stood there for a moment, staring into Chief Bryant's smoldering eyes, and then she turned and left his house, her mission accomplished but her war far from won.

Ki, aboard a big-barreled buckskin he had rented at the livery in McAlester, hailed Luke Hodges as he rode up to the open pit mine where Hodges was supervising the extraction of coal from the sloping side of a denuded hill.

"What brings you back out here, Ki?" Hodges asked as his visitor rode up to him and dismounted.

"Daniel Marshal was giving a little speech in town this morning," Ki explained. "It seems he and a bunch of other fellows are fixing to raise Cain at one or more of the coal mines around McAlester. Jessie asked me if I'd ride on out here and give you fair warning that there might be trouble ahead for you and your men today."

Hodges muttered an oath under his breath. "That Daniel Marshal is more damn trouble than he's worth. Did he say he was coming here?"

Ki shook his head. "No, but he might. He's playing his cards pretty close to his vest as to which mine he means to target."

"What's he planning to do to whichever mine he hits?"

"He didn't say."

"Well, we'll get ready just in case he decides to show up here." Hodges cupped his hands around his mouth and yelled, "Cassidy!"

A man standing at a slant on the slope of the open pit mine glanced over his shoulder, his pick suspended in midair. When Hodges beckoned to him, he dropped his pick and came skidding down the sloping surface of exposed coal. When he hit bottom, he was still on his feet. He hurried over to where Hodges and Ki were standing.

"This is a friend of Miss Starbuck's, Cassidy," Hodges said. "His name is Ki. He came out here to warn me that Daniel Marshal might be planning to attack us."

"Marshal's up to his old tricks, is he now?" Cassidy said with a gleam in his eye.

"It would appear so," Hodges said.

"When do you think the boyo will put in an appearance, Mr. Hodges?"

"I don't know. Do you, Ki?"

"Marshal told the men he was preaching to that they should all meet in McAlester at two o'clock. From there, I assume they'll head out this way."

"Two o'clock," Cassidy repeated. "That gives us more than enough time to get ready for them."

"Cassidy," Hodges said, "I don't want any shooting if it can be avoided."

"Oh, I think it can probably be avoided. We boyos can take care of ourselves without resorting to guns at the drop of a hat. Especially us Irishers. We've got our picks and our shovels, which should stand us in good stead if the going gets heavy. Till then we can use our built-in weapons."

"Built-in weapons?" Ki prompted.

"Dukes," Cassidy said with a grin as he held up his clenched fists. "Boots," he added, doing a little jig to display his booted feet. "You don't know it, of course, Mr. Ki, but me and some of the other Irish fellows working upslope, we come from New York City, which as you may or may not know is truly a rough-and-tumble sort of town. But we all managed to survive there. Some of us even prospered. You see, Mr. Ki, most of us Irish lads have been fighting since the day we was weaned back on the old sod. Fighting comes as natural to an Irishman as does the blessed light of each new day. Fighting's bred in our bones and blood. Some do say it's bred in our very souls."

Ki smiled and nodded. "I've heard something to that effect said more than once."

"Then, too," Cassidy said, pointing to the open pit mine, "we've got the coal itself that is easy to hand. Back in Ireland we were known to throw a brick now and then when the fighting got too hot to handle with fists and feet alone. The bricks we threw—Irish confetti, we called them."

Cassidy bent over, slapped his thighs, and laughed heartily. "We've no bricks here, but the coal'll do nicely."

Hodges gave Cassidy instructions on how the men were to be deployed. Some of them were to be stationed on top of the slope as lookouts. The others were to be positioned on all four sides of the open pit mine with picks and shovels. The narrow pass that led to the mine was to be blocked with some of the wagons that were used to haul coal to the railroad.

When two o'clock came and went with no sign of any of Marshal's men, Cassidy called down from the top of the slope to Hodges and Ki far below him, " 'Tis a false alarm we're having, gents, or so it would appear."

Hodges ordered him and the other miners to remain where they were.

It was almost two-thirty when one of the lookouts shouted to the others, "Riders coming this way. From the east."

"It does begin to look like we're the ones Marshal and his men have picked to make trouble for today," Hodges said to Ki.

Before Ki could respond, Daniel Marshal and several other men climbed up into the beds of the wagons blocking the pass and Marshal yelled, "We're taking over your mine, Hodges. We'll give you and your miners five minutes to clear out. If you're not gone by then, there'll be hell to pay, I promise you."

★

Chapter 5

"You're not giving me orders, Marshal!" Hodges yelled back. "Nor are you and your men going to take so much as a single lump of coal away from me. This mine and the coal in it belongs to me, and I protect what's mine, Marshal, from the likes of you and the other thieves you brought along to back you up, you son of a bitch!"

"You've asked for it, Hodges," Marshal bellowed, "and you're going to get it."

At a signal from Marshal, the men with him raced to attack the miners, who were standing their ground, cudgels and clubs in their hands.

Hodges went racing into the midst of the melee, and within seconds he had sent one of the interlopers sprawling on the ground, where Cassidy finished him off by slamming a shovel down on the top of his head.

Ki ducked as a missile—he wasn't sure what it was—went sailing past his head. He saw it land—a large, jagged piece of coal—and split into fragments on the ground. He wasn't sure who had thrown it. Nor was he sure it had been thrown at him. But he was sure he wasn't going to let it happen again if he could help it. He ran toward several men who were approaching the mine in the distance—the direction the potentially deadly missile had just come from.

"Here comes one of them!" one of the group yelled as Ki neared them. "Get him, boys!"

The men toward whom Ki was heading raised the weapons in their hands and stood their ground as Ki came closer to them. He saw through an irritating haze of coal dust, which was being stirred up by the battling men, a stick of wood in the hand of one man, an ax handle minus its head in the hand of another one, and a rock in the hand of a third.

He also saw the angry expressions on all three men's faces, the expressions that spoke to him of the lust to hurt, perhaps kill, anyone they considered to be their enemy.

He strode into the midst of the men, dodging their blows, both his hands and feet flying. One of his feet, which was raised a good four feet off the ground, caught one of the attackers under the chin, snapping his head backward, and another foot, moments later, plowed deep into the soft belly of an overweight man who was about to club him with the stick he had in his hand. Ki's hands chopped and sliced, sliced and chopped, with the result that two of the men went down in rapid succession and the third turned and ran, dropping his rock as he did so.

Ki turned swiftly. He saw the man coming up behind Hodges with a knife in his hand. He ran toward the pair. His entire body left the ground when he was five feet from Hodges's assailant, whose knife was up in the air and poised for a deadly descent. Ki's crooked right leg shot straight out with the savage force of a sledge and slammed into the back of Hodges's attacker's thick neck. The stunned man flew forward, the knife falling from his hand, and collided with the startled Hodges, who had not known what was about to happen behind his back as he struggled with another of Daniel Marshal's invaders.

"Here," Ki said to Hodges, bending down and retrieving the knife that had belonged to the man he had knocked unconscious and who lay unmoving on the ground. "You might need this." He handed the knife to Hodges.

The mine operator yelled, "Behind you, Ki!"

But Ki turned seconds too late to avoid the two-handed blow that came from a man with fire in his eyes. The man's hands landed on Ki's shoulders with such force that his knees buckled and he fell to the ground. The man seized him by the hair and hauled him to his feet. He began to run with the dazed Ki toward a tree growing not far away.

Hodges went after him, the knife in his hand glinting in the sunlight. A slash of the blade and blood streaked the left arm of the man who was about to ram Ki's head into the trunk of the tree.

Hodges's action made the man lose his grip on Ki. But only for a moment. The man immediately seized a fistful of Ki's hair again and was about to slam his head into the tree when Ki, positioning his right leg in front of him, raised both hands and pushed against the man, who still had a grip on his hair, in the classic "pushing the door" attack of the *Ninja* warrior. He followed through with his left hand, gripping the man's left arm and forcing it upward to a point where it was harmless. Then, with his left arm, the *soe-te* or "entangling arm," still raised, his right arm, called the *mu-te* or "striking arm," pushed against the brawny chest of the man he was battling.

The man successfully resisted Ki until Ki crossed his opponent's left arm above his right arm to render him helpless with the disabling movement called *juji-uke*. His actions succeeded in unbalancing his opponent and shoving him to one side.

Hodges hit the man with a right uppercut and then a sharp left jab before he could recover either his balance or his wits. The man sighed, shuddered, and went down.

Ki and Hodges exchanged satisfied glances, and then both men continued the fight, Ki using *Ninja* techniques to disable one after the other opponent, Hodges swinging the shovel in his hands from right to left and back again as he untiringly attacked any man who tried to stop him.

Coal dust filled the air to such an extent that it turned the golden sun pale, dimming its bright light. Shouts and curses also filled the air. Figures of men, ghostly in the reduced light and clouds of swirling coal dust, lunged, feinted, and struck at one another, some with weapons, others with their bare fists.

Ki, his body spinning in midair as he leaped upward, struck with first one foot and then the other at a man who was coming toward him with a pick. He brought the man down, but then he himself fell as a miner came tumbling head over heels down the slope, knocking Ki's legs out from under him.

The man he had just downed grunted and sprang to his feet. As he reached for the pick he had dropped, Ki scrambled along the ground and got to it first. Ki flung it from the man, and it went soaring down the slope to crash against the wall of Hodges's shed far below.

The man facing Ki cursed and lunged for him. Ki got to his knees, brought both stiffly outstretched arms straight up, and then flung them outward, knocking the man's reaching arms aside. He sprang to his feet and seized the man's left wrist with both hands. Jerking the man toward him while simultaneously bending forward, he threw the man over his head. He turned and watched him strike the ground and then go rolling helplessly down the slope.

Below him, Hodges was gripping his shovel in both hands as he held it in a horizontal position and used it to deflect the blows of another shovel being wielded as a weapon by one of Marshal's men. Hodges managed to hold the other man at bay for some time and avoid being struck, but then his opponent swung his shovel with all his might and it split the wooden handle of Hodges's shovel in two. The now-weaponless Hodges took a step backward and ducked as the man facing him brought his shovel up and then down in a vicious arc. Hodges's maneuver came too late. The man's shovel struck him a blow on the side of his head, and he fell to the ground in a senseless heap.

As the man who had struck him raised the shovel in his hands to hit Hodges again—perhaps fatally this time—Ki went into action. He raced down the slope, the loose coal shifting underfoot and making his progress both erratic and unsteady. He almost fell at one point but managed, with arms whirling wildly in the air, to regain his balance and race onward.

He reached the man with the shovel not a moment too soon. As the tool continued its descent, Ki tackled the wielder of the deadly weapon. Both men went down, turning over and over as they rolled down the slope, their arms locked around one

70

another, the shovel on the ground above them.

When they reached the bottom of the slope, Ki released his hold on the man he had tackled and sprang to his feet. As the man also rose, his meaty hands reaching, Ki kicked out with his left foot, his body twisted sharply to the right. His foot slammed into the man's face, breaking his nose, which immediately began to spout bright red blood that colored the front of his shirt and the coal under his feet.

He screamed, his hands clawing at his face and succeeding only in causing himself more pain and increasing the flow of blood from his broken nose. He backed away, his wide eyes focused on Ki, fear dancing in them. Then he turned and fled.

Ki turned—and was jumped by another of Marshal's men, a beefy, broad-shouldered man built like a barrel.

"I seen what you just done to Jeb," the man snarled and then coughed as coal dust almost choked him. "I'm going to kill you, you bastard you!" He seized Ki by the throat and began to throttle him.

Ki fought desperately to free himself, but the man's hands continued to tighten, not giving a bit. Ki clawed at them until he had drawn blood, but still their grip remained unbroken. He tried kneeing the man in the groin in an effort to free himself, but the man deftly twisted his body to one side so that Ki's knee glanced off his outthrust hip.

The world around Ki, as he struggled to breathe, began to turn pink. Then, red. His throat felt as if it were on fire. His chest heaved as he fought desperately for air. None entered his lungs.

"Jeb was a good man," the man choking Ki muttered. "What's more *he* was an *American*!"

Ki gagged and almost choked to death as the man's fingers tightened their grip. He did the only thing he could do to save himself. He used his thumbs to gouge out the man's eyes. The violent tactic worked; it bought him freedom—and, more importantly, precious air. Ki gulped the air into his burning lungs as his attacker's hands fell away and he screamed as he turned this way and then that, his hands outstretched as he blindly tried to keep his footing. He collided with one of the miners, who drew back his fist and was about to let go with a roundhouse right when he saw the empty, bloody sockets where the man's eyes had been. His fist dropped. So did his lower jaw as he stared aghast at the man's ruined face.

A series of rifle shots sounded.

Ki spun around, searching for the source of the gunfire. He immediately spotted the mounted and uniformed men riding into the area. He counted seven of them. All were heavily armed with both rifles and side arms. More of Daniel Marshal's men? No, he decided. Marshal's supporters wouldn't be wearing uniforms. Then—who?

He was startled then to see that Jessie was riding with the men. He had not seen her at first because she had been riding behind them. But now she was clearly visible to him. He wanted to shout her name, go to her . . .

At that moment, she spotted him standing at the foot of the slope. She spurred her horse and headed toward him.

He didn't wait for her to reach him. Instead, he went sprinting toward her through the roiling clouds of gritty coal dust that the wind was whirling in a westerly direction. At times the dust completely blocked his view of his friend.

"Ki, are you all right?" Jessie cried as she reached him and dismounted.

"I'm all right. A bit battered, that's all. What's going on, Jessie? Who are these men?"

"Choctaw Lighthorsemen."

Ki breathed a sigh of relief. "So it's the Indian police to the rescue."

"I persuaded Chief Bryant to send them out here to prevent this free-for-all, but I see we got here too late."

More shots sounded, and then the leader of the Lighthorsemen shouted an order.

"Stop fighting!"

No one paid any attention to him. The fighting continued, fiercer than before if anything.

The Lighthorse leader signaled to his men. They spread out, all of them still in the saddle. With a display of expert horsemanship, they moved into the midst of the miners who were still battling Marshal's men. Skillfully using their horses and their rifle barrels, they began to separate the two opposing forces. It was slow going. Each pair or group of men had to be literally prodded apart. But prodded apart they all ultimately were until, after nearly ten tense minutes had elapsed, the two sides were standing apart and glaring at one another.

Luke Hodges, who was standing with his miners and being supported by one of them, left the man whose arm was around his waist and made his slow and unsteady way over to where Ki and Jessie were standing.

"Luke, you're hurt!" Jessie exclaimed when she saw the blood on his right temple.

"I might have been dead had it not been for the swift and efficient help of your friend," he responded wryly. "I thank you very much, Ki, for coming to my aid. One of my men saw you come to my rescue and told me about what you did."

"How are you feeling?" Ki asked.

"Wobbly. A little the worse for wear. But I'll recover." Hodges turned his attention to the mounted Lighthorsemen who had positioned themselves between the opposing sides in the distance. "Where did they come from, can anybody tell me?" he asked. "I regained consciousness and there they were riding in among us like avenging angels."

"I persuaded Chief Bryant to send them out to the coal fields," Jessie said. "When we saw none of Daniel Marshal's men at the other mines, we came here and found the battle raging."

"You came just in time," Hodges commented. "If that fight had gone on much longer . . ." His words trailed away as he surveyed both sides' battered and bloody men.

"I would have been here sooner, but I ran into some trouble," Jessie told him.

"Trouble?" Ki prodded.

"Chief Bryant told me I was welcome to take a contingent of his policemen to the coal fields to break up any disturbance that might occur out here. But, when I went to the headquarters of the Lighthorse, Captain Samuels—that's him over there on the bay gelding—refused to come with me. He didn't believe me when I told him that Chief Bryant had given me permission to bring some of his policemen out here to keep the peace. He claimed the chief would never have done such a thing—meaning, act against a fellow Choctaw Indian—Daniel Marshal.

"I finally persuaded Captain Samuels to accompany me back to Chief Bryant's residence, where the chief ordered Samuels and his men to ride out here with me."

"Better late than never," Hodges commented with the ghost of a grin.

"Miss Starbuck, may I have a word with you?"

Jessie looked up to find that Captain Samuels had joined them. "Certainly. What's on your mind, Captain?"

"What do you wish me to do with Mr. Marshal and his men? Do you want them arrested?"

"No, I don't. I think the fact that you and your men put in an appearance and stopped the fighting will serve as sufficient warning to Marshal to mind his manners in the future. But I would be most grateful to you, Captain, if you would disperse those men so they'll not be able to resume their depredations."

Captain Samuels touched the brim of his hat to Jessie before turning his horse and riding back to rejoin his men.

Jessie, Ki, and Hodges stood silently watching as the Lighthorsemen formed a long line and began to walk their horses slowly and relentlessly toward Marshal and his men.

For several minutes, Marshal and his men stood their ground, but then, as the horses came closer—almost nose-to-nose with them—they broke ranks and fell back in the face of the nonviolent onslaught. Minutes later, they were in full rout, running in every direction as fast as they could, away from the mine, and finally disappearing.

Captain Samuels shifted in his saddle so that he could see Jessie. Again he touched the brim of his hat to her.

She waved to him, and then he and his men rode out and also disappeared.

"Well, I guess it's time we got back to work," Hodges said. "Those of us who are still able-bodied, that is."

"I think it would be a good idea, Luke," Jessie said thoughtfully, "if you posted guards around the mine. A lookout up there on that ridge might also be in order. What do you think?"

"My plan exactly. I intend to see to it right now."

"I hope you'll have no more trouble out here."

"Jessie," Ki said, "you spoke too soon. Look!"

Jessie and Hodges both looked in the direction Ki was pointing. Both of them saw the thin tendrils of smoke rising in the distance.

"Fire!" Hodges exclaimed. "It looks like Marshal's men have set the coal afire over there!"

They ran in the direction of the smoke. Before they got to it, they saw the first of the flames flickering skyward from the spot where a portion of the Hodges coal deposit was burning.

Hodges called to his men, many of whom were already heading for the same spot. "Get buckets!" he bellowed. "Get a wagon and drive it down to the river. Fill the buckets with water, load them in the wagon, and bring them back here as fast as you can."

As many of his miners whirled around and set about carrying out their employer's orders, Hodges shouted, "*Go!*" at them, although the order was unnecessary, because already a wagon was hurtling toward the river that flowed behind the mine's stark slope.

"There are tarpaulins in the shed," he told Jessie and Ki as the fire began to spread, flames licking in an almost indolent way along the jagged black surface of the coal. "We can use them to try to smother the flames."

All three raced down the slope to the shed and emerged moments later with tarpaulins in their arms. They ran without speaking back to where the fire was burning, its flames yards high now, and began to flail at the flames with the tarpaulins, sending puffs of smoke up into the air as they did so.

The flames would die down under the attack and then flare up again as soon as the tarps were removed. Sweat coated the trio's faces as they frantically tried to smother the flames. They were still at it when the first of the miners appeared with buckets of water in their hands, which they threw on the flames.

Steam hissed in the air. Smoke swarmed over the open pit, making it hard for the firefighters to breathe or see clearly. But they fought on, the bucket brigade they had formed working at top speed. The heat of the fire came at them in hot waves, almost hot enough to sear exposed portions of their skin.

"Give me your tarp," Ki said to Jessie. When she handed it to him, he seized a bucket of water from one of the men in the bucket brigade and emptied it onto the tarp before handing it back to Jessie, who valiantly swatted the flames with the soaked tarp, which was now heavy in her hands.

Ki soaked his own tarp and then handed it to Hodges in exchange for the one Hodges had been using.

The tarps proved far more effective wet than they had while dry. The trio managed to put out a large portion of the fire while the rest of the firefighters continued to pour water on the flames that still remained.

Jessie let out a cry of alarm as her hair was singed by an isolated flame and almost caught fire. It didn't only because she had the presence of mind to cover her head with her wet tarp. Then she resumed her battle with the flames, with Ki working on her right side and Hodges working off to her left.

The harsh sounds of men coughing blended with the equally harsh crackle of the flames. Smoke was everywhere. Occasionally, piles of coal dust ignited with a *whoosshh* as the fire reached them. They sent fingers of flame clawing at the sky, which the thick smoke had darkened. Embers flew through the air. A man screamed in pain as some of them landed on him, igniting his shirt and forcing him to roll on the ground to extinguish the devouring flames.

"A circle!" Hodges shouted, his voice cracking as a result of the rawness of his smoke-coated throat's membranes. "Make a circle around the fire!"

His men promptly obeyed him. They scurried to form the circle and never for a second stopped passing water from one man to the next. When the circle was completed, Hodges turned and shouted, "Hurry!" to the wagon loaded with filled buckets of water, which was almost invisible as it made its way toward the fire.

When it arrived, he and Ki leaped into its bed and began handing down buckets of water to the miners, who now formed a nearly perfect circle as they continued to do battle with the blaze that was close to being out of control.

Men danced forward, threw their water on the flames and then leaped backward as scalding steam rose and threatened to sear their skin. Then they repeated the process, a few of them visibly beginning to tire as a result of their prolonged and arduous efforts.

As Hodges shouted words of encouragement to them, they responded by fighting even harder, their faces blackened with soot and the whites of their eyes reddened by the irritating smoke.

"It's working!" Jessie cried, blinking the sweat out of her eyes as she continued to flail at the fire with her tarp. "It's out over here!"

She moved to her right and continued her efforts, sweat falling from her face into some small flames at her feet. All around her, the miners, Ki, and Hodges worked as feverishly as she did, and some time later, after the passage of what to Jessie seemed like an eternity, it was over. The last of the flames were doused with water by the members of the bucket brigade or smothered by her and Ki and Hodges, whose scorched tarpaulins now had numerous holes burned in them.

She straightened up, feeling in her back and arms aches that had not been there before her firefighting efforts began. She dropped her tarp and, placing her hands in the small of her back, bent backward to try to rid her body of the kinks it had taken on during the past long minutes. Minutes? Maybe so. But to her those minutes had seemed like hours.

"You all right, Jessie?" Hodges asked, his voice still husky.

She gave him a reassuring smile and nodded.

He reached out and tenderly touched her sweat-slick cheek. "Thanks for pitching in, you and Ki, the way you did."

"I had to protect my business interests," Jessie responded.

"You could have left the battle to us fellows," Hodges told her. "You could have stood on the sidelines and watched."

"Jessie stand on the sidelines?" Ki asked in mock horror. "That will never happen. She'll always and forever be right in the thick of whatever's going on, be it fire or fracas or Fourth of July celebration."

"You're not burnt, are you?" Hodges inquired as he put an arm around her waist to steady her.

"No, I'm fine. Really I am. Well, not altogether fine, I guess. What I really am is angry. Mad as a hatter if the truth's to be told."

"About the fire?"

"Yes. The fight and the fire. I intend to pay Mr. Daniel Marshal a visit and give him a piece—and not a pleasant

77

piece—of my mind. If he should ever dare try anything like this again, I'll—"

"Bite your tongue, Jessie," Ki cautioned. Then, turning to Hodges, he said, "I notice that some of your miners look a little the worse for wear. When I get back to town, I'll stop at the doctor's office and tell him he needs to take a trip out here, where he'll find a whole passel of patients waiting for him to attend to."

"I'd appreciate that," Hodges said. "I'd go myself, but I've got to stay here and keep an eye on things. Coal's a funny thing. Once it starts to burn, you can never be one hundred percent sure it's altogether out. At least, not for a while, you can't. I've known of cases where fires started in underground coal mines and no matter what folks did to douse them, some of them were still smoldering as long as a year after they started. You could see smoke coming up out of fissures in the ground like the Devil was having a clambake down there in his domain."

"Keep your eyes and ears open," Jessie advised him. "I wouldn't put it past Marshal to pull some other stunt like that fire he set."

"If he does, I'll be ready for it—and for him, too," Hodges assured her, his eyes glinting.

With that, Jessie and Ki went to their horses. After swinging into their saddles and waving good-bye to Hodges and his miners, they rode out, heading for town.

By the time they got there, Jessie was still fuming. During their ride, she had made up her mind that while Ki went to get the doctor to attend to the injured men at the mine, she would pay a visit to the town's marshal. She would not even take time to return to the hotel and bathe before doing so. Her vanity would have to be set aside until she had taken care of the matter that was uppermost on her mind at the moment—pressing charges against Daniel Marshal and the men he had led to Luke Hodges's mine. Among the charges: assault, battery, and arson.

"I'll be stopping off here," Ki told her as they approached the doctor's office, which was on the second floor of a building that housed a drugstore on the ground floor.

"I'll see you later at the hotel."

As Jessie rode on, Ki drew rein, dismounted, and left his horse at the hitchrail in front of the drugstore. He climbed the stairs on the side of the building and obeyed the sign in the window of the door at the top of them, which said, Walk In.

"Is the doctor in?" he asked the woman in the doctor's reception room.

"Yes, sir, but he's with a patient. Have you an appointment?"

"No, and I don't need one. I just came by to get word to the doctor that there's been trouble out at the Hodges mine. Some men have been hurt in a fistfight and a fire that just took place out there. He'd better head out there just as soon as he can. Will you be good enough to give him my message?"

"Yes, sir, of course I will."

Ki turned and left. He led his horse to the livery barn and left it there with instructions to the farrier to grain and water the animal. In answer to the man's question, he said, yes, he might be needing the horse again. The farrier promised to hold the animal for him—if he paid for the privilege. Ki did and then went to the canvas-enclosed area, directly behind the barber shop, that served as a public bathhouse.

Jessie strode back and forth in front of the desk behind which McAlester's marshal was seated in the cramped little office.

"They came out there to the mine that Luke Hodges leases from me and they attacked the miners like some sort of wild animals and then they set the mine on fire. It's a wonder one or more of them wasn't killed during the attack. The unprovoked attack, I hasten to add."

"Well, Miss Starbuck," the marshal drawled after removing a wooden toothpick from his mouth, "I wouldn't come right out and say that this here attack you're talking about was what you could call unprovoked."

Jessie halted in mid-stride and stood staring incredulously at the marshal. "You dare to suggest that Luke Hodges or his employees provoked the attack Daniel Marshal and his men launched against them?"

"I'm not so sure I'm suggesting anything, Miss Starbuck, What I was doing—you might call it wondering. That's right. Wondering."

Jessie forced herself to remain calm. "What was it you were *wondering* about, Marshal?"

"The Choctaws are pretty hot under the collar right now about the way the Nation's filling up with all kinds of people who aren't Indians and who are running businesses of one kind or another or farming land that they've got no legal claim to and the like. The Choctaws, they call such people—both Negroes and whites—intruders. Miss Starbuck, Chief Bryant, maybe he has a point when he says the miners around McAlester are intruders."

"That's absolutely preposterous!" Jessie cried. She bent down, placed her knuckles on the desk, and added, "As far as I know, all the people who are running mining operations in the Choctaw coal fields have valid contracts with the tribe—contracts signed by none other than Chief Joseph Bryant himself—that give them permission to do what they're doing. So how in the world can you sit there and suggest to me that the people who own, operate, and staff the mines are intruders?"

"I told you before, Miss Starbuck, I don't think I'm suggesting anything. It's not me that's saying you and the other mine owners and the people you lease your mines to and the men who work them are intruders. That's the position taken by a lot of Indians these days."

"And you're saying that you think the men who attacked Luke Hodges and his men had a right to do what they did simply because some Choctaws now choose to consider them intruders in their territory, is that it?"

"That's about the size of it."

Jessie drew several deep breaths before trusting herself to continue. "That does not give them the right to attack people."

"Miss Starbuck, did you bring any witnesses with you who can testify to what you say happened out at the Hodges outfit?"

"No. But I can get some—many, as a matter of fact."

"What do you reckon will happen if Daniel Marshal up and denies an attack even took place out there?"

"We can prove that it did take place. But you're putting the cart before the horse, Marshal. That matter will be dealt with when we go to trial. Right now what I came here to ask you to do is to arrest Marshal and any of the men who sided with him this afternoon at the Hodges mine."

"I can't do that. Not without some kind of proof, I can't. If I went around arresting everybody in this town who's been accused of something or other on account of somebody's got a grudge against them, I'd have to build me a new jail. *Two* new jails!"

"Marshal, I simply cannot believe what I'm hearing from you."

"Oh, I'll ask around about what you say happened. I'll talk to Dan Marshal. Hear what he has to say about things. Maybe I can even find somebody or other who'll admit to being out at the Hodges mine with him today. I'll let you know what I find out—if I find out anything at all."

"You sound to me like you're practically in cahoots with Daniel Marshal," Jessie declared heatedly.

The marshal shot to his feet and wagged an index finger in Jessie's face. "Watch your step, woman! I'm paid to keep the peace in this town—"

"My point exactly."

"And I'll arrest you to do it if you keep going about and making unproved accusations against solid citizens of Choctaw Nation."

"You're speaking, I suppose, of Daniel Marshal."

"I am indeed."

Jessie straightened up. She stood there for a moment glaring at the lawman facing her. Then she turned on her heels and left his office, knowing she had been summarily dismissed and furious about that fact.

Ki climbed out of the tin tub, which was full of dirty water and just-as-dirty soap suds, and began to dry himself with the towel the bathhouse attendant had given him when he arrived.

He was dressing when he heard one of the other men in the establishment say, "She's got tits like two ripe pumpkins and a twat as tight as a new pair of boots."

"You had her, did you?" another man asked as both of them soaked in their respective tubs.

"Yep. Twice. She just came to work in Madame Harley's parlor house a week ago, but already just about every man in town has heard about her and most of them have had her. She's French, Marie is, or so she says. She certainly knows how to do the things the French are famous for."

"Excuse me, sir," Ki said as he continued dressing. "Can you tell me the location of Madame Harley's parlor house? I'm new in town and have never been there."

"You bet," replied the man who had spoken first. He gave Ki the address he was seeking.

"Much obliged to you," Ki said as he finished dressing and paid the attendant.

"If you're going to Madame Harley's place," said the man who had extolled the virtue of the parlor house's newest addition, "ask for Marie. She'll show you a trick or two that'll curl your toes and stiffen your dick for sure."

Ki nodded and left the bathhouse. Despite his eagerness to make the acquaintance of the woman named Marie, he went first to the McAlester Arms, where he changed clothes. Then he left the hotel and made his way to the address he had been given in the bathhouse.

When he arrived and knocked on the oak door, he was welcomed by a big-bosomed woman with lush red hair, who invited him in and asked him if he wanted to buy a drink.

"No, ma'am—"

"Let's be friends instead of formal. My name is Mrs. Harley. What's yours?"

"Ki."

"Chinese?"

"Japanese."

Mrs. Harley arched an inquisitive eyebrow and asked, "Japanese, huh? Do you people do it the American way or different?"

"That depends."

"I won't ask on what. Do you want to meet the girls now?"

Ki shook his head. "I came to call on Marie."

"My, oh, my but that girl is a wonder. She's been in town but a week, and already she has every man around asking after her. She's in room four at the top of the stairs. That'll be two dollars, please."

Ki dug the money out of his trousers and placed it in Mrs. Harley's outstretched hand. "Top of the stairs, you say."

"That's right. Have a good time up there."

I sure do hope to, Ki thought as he climbed the stairs and knocked on the door of room number four.

"Well, hello there," the woman who opened the door purred, reaching out and placing a soft hand on his shoulder. "I'm Marie. Come in."

She stepped aside and Ki entered the room, which was furnished with little more than a big brass bed.

"What's your pleasure?" Marie asked him, placing both hands on his shoulders this time and tickling his ear lobes.

"The usual."

Marie smiled charmingly. "The usual isn't the usual—not when you do it with me, it isn't."

Ki put his arms around Marie and drew her to him. He kissed her hard on her lips, desire already raging within him. It raged even more wildly as she took his thrusting tongue into her mouth and began to suck on it.

As their kiss continued, Ki slipped her blouse down over her shoulders to bare her breasts, which he proceeded to fondle. He heard her moan and felt her arms tighten on him.

When their kiss ended a moment later, he practically ripped the blouse from her body. Within minutes, they were both naked and lying side by side on the bed, their arms enfolding one another, their lips and hands exploring.

Ki reached down and cupped Marie's moist mound. Massaging it, he continued kissing her face, neck, ears. Then he slid the middle finger of his right hand into her, and she groaned aloud as it plunged deeper. It twisted and turned in its eager explorations, causing her to twist and turn with pleasure.

Ki's erection throbbed against her thigh and she pressed herself against it. As she did so, her juices began to soak his probing finger. He withdrew it and rolled over on top of her. She cried out in sensual delight when his shaft began to plow the path his finger had previously taken.

He groaned with pleasure and arched his back. Slowly, he began to move upon her. He kissed her forehead and then her lips. He gradually increased the tempo of his movements, rising and falling upon Marie in a rhythm that made her cry out in ecstasy and toss her head from side to side. As she writhed

83

with pleasure beneath him, he raised himself up on his hands so that he could look down and watch the series of emotions flitting across her face.

Watching her closely and listening to her little yelps of pleasure, he brought her to the brink of a climax. Then, with deft movements, he eased her back down from the thrilling peak she had reached.

He began to buck even faster and with much more passion, causing her to climax.

He continued plunging into her, almost violently now, and she began to shudder so much that the brass bed shook and its springs screamed. The second time she came, a few minutes later, she gave a short series of grunts, her head tossing wildly.

His hips began to pound her, and she seemed to be reveling in the pounding. A moment later Ki flooded her, his body convulsing in a series of spasms as ecstasy seized and shook him.

Then, as both of their bodies calmed, Marie took his head in her hands and kissed him full on the lips. "*Très bien*," she murmured languidly.

"It was indeed very good," Ki agreed with a sigh of contentment.

★

Chapter 6

Jessie stopped an elderly man outside the marshal's office and asked him if he knew where Daniel Marshal lived.

"Why, sure, I do, ma'am. Everybody in town, seems like, knows Danny. He's what you could call our local hero. A hometown boy trying to make good."

Jessie wanted to ask the man if hometown boys in McAlester made good by setting fire to coal fields owned by somebody else. But she said nothing, not wanting to alienate the man and possibly cause him to refuse to give her the information she was seeking.

"Danny lives out on the Post Road, which is a funny name for the place since it's nothing more than a cowpath through the woods out near the Crossroads. You'll find it easy enough. It's a long house built Indian style. What some are pleased to call 'two pens and a passage.' "

"Thank you for the information."

As Jessie made her way to the hitchrail next door where she had left her horse, the man called out to her.

"You tell Danny old Pat Farley said howdy. Tell him when

you see him I said he did good lighting that fire under those intruders out there at the Hodges mine. Tell him I said it's just too bad it didn't work. Most folks round here would have liked to see those intruders run out of the coal fields on a rail while all dolled up in nothing else but hot tar and fluttery feathers."

Jessie swung into the saddle without saying a word, although there were a number of words, most of them decidedly unlady-like, roiling in her brain. She rode down the street thinking that the sentiment in McAlester seemed to be decidedly in favor of men like Daniel Marshal and against the miners working the coal fields. That knowledge not only made her uneasy, it worried her. It suggested to her that the incident at the coal fields earlier that day might well be but the beginning battle in what could become a protracted—and perhaps lethal—war between people like herself on one side and who-knew-how-many Indians and their white sympathizers on the other.

It was late in the afternoon when she reached the Cross-roads, which was the spot not far from McAlester where the legendary California Trail from Fort Smith, Arkansas, crossed the much older Texas Road. The California Trail had been traveled by thousands of prairie schooners that had taken the gold-seeking forty-niners to the fabled land of the setting sun, where they hoped to wring their fortune from the earth.

Jessie was surprised to see that the Katy railroad was hard at work laying track almost precisely upon the Texas Road itself. She drew rein beside the men working on the line and asked what they were doing.

A man with a round red face and blue eyes that twinkled like those of an elf doffed his hat to her and replied, "Ma'am, we're building another spur line out over thataway."

Jessie glanced in the direction he had pointed. "But why?" she asked. "There's no town that I know of over there."

"You speak the gospel truth, ma'am," the man declared. "But it's not a town we're building to. It's another open pit mine that just opened over thataway."

Jessie bade the man good-bye and rode on until she spotted the log house that her informant in McAlester had referred to as "two pens and a passage."

It resembled two small log cabins connected by a covered

passage. Was this the lair of Daniel Marshal? She intended to find out. She rode up to the building and dismounted. She left her horse ground-hitched and knocked on the door of the cabin on her left.

She knocked again, the door of the cabin on her right opened, and Marshal appeared and stared at her in surprise.

Just like him, she found herself thinking. I look for him in one place, and out of sheer perversity, he appears in another. She knew she was being absurd thinking the way she was, but she couldn't seem to help it.

"What do you want?" Marshal barked.

"What do I want?" Jessie faced him with her hands on her hips and her legs planted far apart. "I want you to stop making trouble for a business partner of mine."

"You're talking about Luke Hodges."

"I am."

"You're wasting your time and your breath. Go away, Miss Starbuck. I've got nothing to say to you."

"Well, I have one or two things to say to you, Mr. Marshal, although I usually do not make a habit of holding conversations with arsonists."

Marshal's eyes narrowed. "What are you talking about?"

"You know damn well what I'm talking about. I'm talking about the fire you set, you and your men, out at the Hodges mine."

"I set no fire. And as far as I know, none of my men did either."

"You'd better keep closer tabs on them, then, if you truly don't know they set the fire."

"What was burnt?"

Jessie was about to give Marshal a sarcastic reply, which she thought his question warranted, when the thought occurred to her that maybe he was telling the truth. Maybe he really did not know about the fire.

"The coal was set afire," she finally said, watching Marshal carefully.

He showed genuine surprise at her answer, which made her think that he was either telling the truth or else he was an actor of consummate skill.

"We did not go out to the mine to cause such damage," he

87

said. "In fact, we hoped not even to have to fight your men."

"Luke Hodges's men," Jessie corrected.

Marshal shrugged the remark away. "Right from the start, we gave the miners a choice," he pointed out. "They could throw down their tools and leave peacefully and that would be that, or they could refuse to do so, in which case we would do our level best to drive them away. They refused to leave. So we fought."

"They'll continue to fight," Jessie declared. "For their jobs and for the food those jobs put in their mouths and the mouths of their families. So be warned, Mr. Marshal. If you should try a repeat performance of today's event, we'll be ready for you, and next time you might not get off so lightly."

"I'm not giving up," Marshal declared with his jaw set and an obstinate look in his eyes.

"Neither am I," Jessie quickly assured him.

"I won't quit until my people, the Choctaws, have full, complete, and unencumbered possession of the coal fields which rightfully belong to them."

Jessie, who had turned and started to walk away, halted and turned back to face Marshal, anger flashing in her eyes. "What then, Mr. Marshal? Let's assume for the moment that you succeed in your violent endeavors to take over the mines—"

"I have already told you I neither arranged for, nor do I condone, the arson you just told me about," he interrupted.

Ignoring him, Jessie continued, "As I was saying, if you persist in your chancy maneuvers, you may well live to rue the day you ever embarked upon them. What do you think would happen, Mr. Marshal, if your efforts met with success?"

Without pausing long enough to allow him to answer her question, Jessie hurried on. "You and I both know that the Choctaws do not now and have never worked the mines, nor have they ever wanted to do so. Your people, Mr. Marshal, consider such labor demeaning and quite beneath them. That is one of the reasons Chief Bryant was delighted when I and Monty Carruthers and others approached him with the proposal that we contract to mine the coal and share the profits thus derived from it with the tribe. If you were to drive us out, who then would work the mines?"

"We would," Marshal said but without strong conviction in

his voice. "The Choctaw people would."

"They have never done so in the past, Mr. Marshal. What makes you think they will do so in the future?"

"When the mines are ours—"

"Nothing will have changed insofar as the attitude of the people of your tribe toward working in a mine is concerned. You will have to hire outsiders to do your dirty work for you. You will thus wind up with a situation not unlike the one you now denounce so enthusiastically at every opportunity."

"I concede the fact that we may face a few problems once the mines are in our hands," Marshal reluctantly admitted. "But they are problems we will solve, I can assure you."

"I must say, quite frankly, you don't sound very convinced of that fact, Mr. Marshal. And in this general connection, what do you or the people who now applaud you so eagerly—by the way, I met one of your admirers in town, a Mr. Pat Farley, who asked to be remembered to you—what will people like your friend, Mr. Farley, have to say when and if the mines are taken over by you and mismanaged as I have little doubt they will be under your misguided aegis?"

"Those are my problems, not yours, Miss Starbuck, and I have no wish to discuss them any further with you at this time."

"And you, Mr. Marshal, are my problem. Let me assure you that I am very good at solving problems. I intend to solve *you*, Mr. Marshal."

"You may have met your match in me. But even if, in your so annoyingly arrogant way, you do find a way to defeat me, what will you do about the others like me who are bound and determined, as am I, to defeat you? I'm talking, for example, about Caleb Pace and your very own miners, who, if Pace has his way, will go on strike and close your mine down completely."

"I told you, Mr. Marshal. I'm good at solving problems."

Marshal muttered something angry and unintelligible before disappearing inside his house.

Jessie had finished bathing in a tin tub in her room and was sitting naked on the edge of her bed drying her hair with a thick towel when a knock sounded on the door.

Ki, she thought as she got up, wrapped the towel around her hair, slipped into a robe, and opened the door. But it was not Ki who was standing outside in the hall.

"This is a surprise, Monty," Jessie said as she admitted him and Leonard Fanshaw of the Katy railroad to her room.

"It appears we've come at an inappropriate time, Jessie," Carruthers said.

"We can come another time that is more convenient for you," Fanshaw said in a silken voice.

"Stay, gentlemen," Jessie said, dismissing their concerns with an airy wave of her hand. "What can I do for you?"

"Jessie, we heard about what happened at your lessee's mine this afternoon," Carruthers said as he sat down in a chair near the door and Fanshaw took a chair near the window. "A truly terrible thing. We were most upset, Leonard and I, and we wanted to come here to see if you were all right."

"We heard terrible stories, Jessie," Fanshaw said. "Someone said you had been raped repeatedly during the assault on the mine."

"Wild rumors always spread after an event like the one that occurred today," Jessie said. "I'm quite all right, although a bit tired."

The two men exchanged concerned glances, after which Fanshaw said, "Monty, we really should go and come back at another time."

"Please stay," Jessie said. "I'm fine actually."

"That is good news," Carruthers said with a sigh. "Leonard and I were both worried about you. As he said, we heard stories—"

"Rumors," Fanshaw interrupted.

"We came to call to find out first of all if you were well, and now that we know you are, we can tell you the good news which we also came here to convey to you if we found you up to talking with us."

"I'm always glad to hear good news. What is it?"

"When we heard what happened today at the Hodges mine," Carruthers began, "we decided to turn an essentially negative occurrence into something positive, if at all possible."

"I am happy to say we were successful in so doing," a

90

smiling Fanshaw declared as he folded his hands across his ample girth.

Jessie looked from one man to the other and then asked, "What exactly is the good news?"

Both men spoke at once, their words garbled. Then, deferring to Carruthers, Fanshaw remained silent as the mine owner said, "When I heard about the violence that had been perpetrated on you and your lessee and his miners, I went at once to Leonard's office here in town and told him that we must do something."

" 'Strike while the iron is hot' is the way you put it," Fanshaw stated.

"Precisely. We both then went to call on Arthur Pryor, the Indian agent. We told him that what Daniel Marshal had done was intolerable and we would not stand for it. We brought with us the contracts each of us had signed in the past with Chief Bryant—Leonard's having to do, of course, with the building of spur lines to the mines, and mine having to do with present and planned development of the coal fields. We showed them to Pryor, who, we knew, was already familiar with them."

"But we thought he would, upon seeing them once again, be suitably impressed," Fanshaw interjected.

"He was," Carruthers announced. "We told him in no uncertain terms that we wanted him to take appropriate action to stop such terrible things from happening and interfering with our mining operations in Choctaw Nation."

"He promised to look into the matter," Fanshaw said. "But that was not nearly good enough for us. We wanted more."

"And we got it," Carruthers said, his eyes glowing as he pulled a folded piece of paper from his coat pocket and waved it at Jessie.

Tweedledum and Tweedledee, she found herself thinking. The two men reminded her of the characters from *Through the Looking Glass*. It had something to do with their similarly ample girths and also with their odd blend of self-satisfaction and belligerence.

"Read this," Carruthers said, rising and handing the paper to Jessie.

Jessie took it from him and sat down on the bed to examine

91

it. She read through the brief paragraphs the paper contained and then read them a second time before looking up at the two men, who were watching her intently.

"What this says, in essence, is that the mine owners named herein, and, I note, I'm one of them—"

"We took the liberty of speaking for you as well as ourselves," a beaming Carruthers declared.

"It says that we, the mine owners and the president of the Missouri, Kansas, and Texas railroad," she glanced at Fanshaw and then back down at the paper in her hands, "have the right, as ratified by the duly appointed representative of the federal government in charge of tribal administration, to do any and all things deemed necessary and/or appropriate to operate coal mines profitably in the Choctaw republic."

"Any and all things," Fanshaw echoed, looking as pleased as a cat lapping cream.

"*Carte blanche* is what we have been given, Jessie," Carruthers crowed. "Isn't that simply marvelous?"

"Simply wonderful?" added Fanshaw, rubbing his pudgy hands together.

Jessie wasn't so sure it was either marvelous or wonderful. She thought it just might be going a bit too far on the part of Agent Pryor.

"That," added Carruthers, pointing to the paper in Jessie's hand, "will most certainly put a burr in the britches of the likes of Daniel Marshal, not to mention Chief Joseph Bryant."

"Most certainly," Fanshaw echoed.

Jessie glanced again at the paper in her hand and then gave it back to Carruthers, who pocketed it. "I'm sure you're both right. That document is not likely to endear the mine owners to Mr. Marshal or to Chief Bryant. If one takes what Mr. Pryor has written at face value, it means that we can get away with just about anything we wish, as long as we can claim that our actions are designed to insure the profitable operation of our mines."

"Precisely," Carruthers said, beaming.

"Just so," said Fanshaw with a pleased smirk.

Jessie hesitated a moment and then said, "I wish you hadn't used my name in that document, gentlemen."

"We thought you would want to be a party to such an

agreement that is so clearly in our best interests, Jessie," a puzzled Carruthers said.

"We took the liberty of using your name as well as our own to buttress your position, Jessie, as well as our own," Fanshaw declared a bit peevishly.

"I understand that. But I would rather not be a party to such a sweeping and, I feel I have to say, unfair arrangement."

The two men in the room exchanged startled glances. Then they both looked back at Jessie. Carruthers was the first to speak. "I must say I think there is nothing unfair at all about that agreement. It merely states that we have the right to do whatever we must to mine the coal we have discovered and, by implication, that we are not to be prevented from doing so."

"It is that latter point, Jessie," Fanshaw said, leaning forward in his chair and shaking an index finger at her in a somewhat schoolmasterish manner, "that is the most important. Why, I have only to think of what happened earlier today at the Hodges mine to rejoice over the fact that we now have something of a club—as represented by that document—to hold over the hot heads of the likes of Daniel Marshal and any other—I hesitate to refer to them as gentlemen—who would do us harm as a result of the misguided ill will they harbor against us."

"I appreciate what you did as well as your motives for doing it," Jessie quickly assured both men. "It's just that I am made distinctly uneasy by what I see as the one-sidedness of the document. It allows us to do just about anything we want and does not take a balanced view of the situation as it presently exists in the coal fields. After all, Daniel Marshal and Chief Bryant have valid points concerning what we do and how we do it and how what we do might be changed."

"You're not suggesting, I trust," Carruthers said with a note of indignation in his voice, "that you think those men are right in wanting to take our mines away from us, are you, Jessie?"

"No, I'm not. But—"

"Jessie, Jessie, Jessie," Fanshaw interrupted, shaking his head, his watery eyes mournful. "Don't you see? Don't you understand what is going on here?"

Jessie stared at him, waiting for him to continue.

"That document is a new and powerful weapon in our arsenal. We can use it against the Daniel Marshals of this world and also the Chief Bryants who are trying to make things difficult for us and costing us money in the process."

"Not to mention endangering our lives and the lives of our employees," Carruthers was quick to add.

"I'm sure Jessie sees my point, Monty," Fanshaw said in a soothing tone. "I'm sure she stands shoulder to shoulder with us in this battle we are all engaged in."

"Of course," Carruthers said. "So let us change the subject. Let us move on to another matter. Jessie, Leonard and I have more good news to tell you."

Jessie was still pondering the "goodness" of the news she had already been given by her visitors when Carruthers added, "We have made arrangements to build a spur line to the new coal deposits my geologists have found and have only yesterday confirmed as worth hundreds of thousands of dollars once mined."

"What do you mean you have made 'arrangements'?" Jessie asked.

"We informed Chief Bryant earlier today of the discovery," Carruthers explained.

"In a personal visit to him," Fanshaw amplified.

"We told him of our intention to build a spur line to the new area south of town so that we may more readily ship coal out of it," Carruthers continued.

"What was the chief's reaction?" Jessie asked.

"Well, he was not overjoyed at the news, I have to say," Carruthers declared. "In fact, he became quite hot under the collar and told us in no uncertain terms that he would not allow even one more spur line to be built in his territory. He also said he would seek an injunction from the Choctaw Legislature to prevent us from mining in the area I mentioned."

"You call all this good news?" a perplexed Jessie inquired.

"Most certainly," Fanshaw answered her. "Chief Bryant will not be the obstacle in the future that he is at the moment. As Monty said, we have made arrangements which involve bypassing him in order to get the permission we need to proceed with our plans."

"How do you plan to bypass the Principal Chief of the Choctaw Nation?" Jessie asked.

It was Carruthers who answered her. "We intend to meet with key members of the Choctaw Legislature and present our case for development of the new coal deposits we've located."

"And the case for building a spur line into the particular area for ease of shipment of the coal mined there," Fanshaw quickly added.

"Wait a minute," Jessie said, her brow furrowing as she thoughtfully weighed what she had been told. "I don't believe the Choctaw Legislature can fly in the face of a decision made by their Principal Chief. Or am I wrong about that?"

"No, you're right, Jessie," Carruthers admitted with evident reluctance. "But consider the matter from this angle. If we are successful in our meetings with the individual legislators, which we have set for tomorrow—successful, that is, with a clear majority of them—then what can Chief Bryant do? Maintain his opposition to our plans in the face of his nation's legislators' approval of it? That hardly seems likely to me. What does seem likely is that Bryant will be forced to back off in the face of the serious split among his own people as represented by the lawmakers of his republic."

"A neat move, don't you think?" a smiling Fanshaw asked Jessie.

"Gentlemen, I don't want to throw cold water on your plans, but let me just say this about them. It seems to me that if you do indeed get the legislature on your side—"

"*Our* side," Fanshaw interrupted pointedly.

"All right. Our side. If you do get them to go along, it seems to me that what you're doing is sowing the seed of even more discontent. There well may be additional forces set into motion by such a move that could, in both the short and the long run, be detrimental to the very interests you are trying to protect."

Carruthers cleared his throat and said with exaggerated patience, "We have handled dissent and opposition in the past. We have continued to mine coal in the face of the rabble-rousing of Daniel Marshal and the complaints of some of the miners who have been listening to the strike talk being spread by Caleb Pace. We have also stood up to Chief Bryant in the past and will continue to do so in the future."

"I admire your courage, Monty," Jessie said, "but I wonder if it wouldn't be better to try some conciliatory moves at this point to smooth things over somewhat."

"Conciliatory moves? What sort of conciliatory moves do you have in mind?"

"Well, we could agree to postpone development of the new deposits you've located until such time as the root issues in our disputes are resolved with the various parties involved."

Carruthers got to his feet and began to stride back and forth in the room, his hands clasped behind his back. "That is all well and good for you to say, Jessie, but the coal deposits we are discussing here are not yours. They're mine. So it is, if you'll forgive me for speaking bluntly, no skin off your nose if they are let lie fallow, so to speak."

"Then let's go about this another way," Jessie suggested. "Let's suspend all operations for a short time. Just long enough to cool things down somewhat. We could use that idle period in the mines to sit down and discuss the problems we have with the Choctaws and, not so incidentally, with our own employees."

"I wouldn't give Caleb Pace the time of day!" Carruthers exclaimed angrily.

"Caleb Pace is just the most obvious of the miners who feel we have wage and safety problems in our mines. We have to bear in mind that he is not the problem. He is merely the voice of the problem. It's not just Caleb Pace we have to deal with. It's our own men."

Carruthers stopped pacing and stood facing Jessie. "I'm not backing off," he stated bluntly. "You've known me for many years, Jessie, so you know I'm not one to run away from a fight. I came here hoping we would be able to present a united front in the face of the many difficulties facing us, but you go ahead and talk to Marshal or Pace or anybody else you feel you have to kowtow to—"

"Monty, that's not fair!" Jessie protested. "I am not suggesting that I or you or any other mine owner kowtow to anybody!"

"I'll take that back then. I'll put it this way. Do what you think you have to do. But don't try to interfere with what I'm doing. The Choctaw coal fields are a bonanza as rich as any gold mine, and I for one do not intend to lose out on that bonanza. I intend to reap its benefits down to the very last dime it has to yield."

Fanshaw rose. "I think it's time we were going, Monty."

Jessie started to protest their departure, but then, realizing she had nothing more to say to them, she saw them out.

She closed the door after they had gone, leaned back against it, and closed her eyes. I tried to dampen down the situation, she thought, taking a deep breath. But instead it seems I've just gone and added more fuel to an already hot fire.

"It sounds to me like Monty Carruthers is one determined man," Ki commented over breakfast the next morning with Jessie.

"Determined times ten, yes," she agreed. "Also stubborn. He won't give an inch. I think it's a matter of self-esteem with him. He thinks to compromise is a sign of weakness."

"Do I understand you to be implying that compromise is a sign of strength?"

"I believe it is, yes. It's not weakness to see another person's opposing point of view and seek some middle ground between it and your own view. That's strength. It takes a person confident about himself to compromise. I suspect the kind of rigidity Carruthers displays is really a wall behind which he hides his own insecurities and uncertainties."

"And Leonard Fanshaw?"

Jessie made a dismissive gesture. "Fanshaw is, let's say it right up front, a very successful businessman. He runs a profitable railroad and has done so for years. But he's shadow in the face of Monty Carruthers's substance."

"What do you mean?"

"Monty's a go-getter. Fanshaw goes along with such a man for his own benefit. If Monty shows him a way to make money, Fanshaw will do everything in his power to make that way succeed with all his skills. But, in the final analysis, it's men like Monty who play the tunes that men like Leonard Fanshaw dance to."

"So it's Carruthers you have to change. If you change him, you'll also change Fanshaw. Is that it?"

"That, in a nutshell, is it, yes."

Ki forked some poached eggs into his mouth and chewed. After swallowing, he said, "Well, what's your next move?"

"I've been thinking of having a talk with Arthur Pryor."

"The Indian agent."

Jessie nodded and drank some coffee, her breakfast only half-eaten and growing cold on her plate. "I'd like to see if I can get Pryor to change his mind about that agreement he made with Monty and Fanshaw."

"Do you think he's likely to do that?"

"I don't really know. But I think Pryor might be a good place to start to try to settle things down a bit around here. You know the Indians—and I'm talking about Indians all over the country, not just the members of the so-called Five Civilized Tribes—do not have a great deal of love for our federal government. They've seen too many treaties dishonored and too many promises broken by our people to their distinct detriment. Pryor, in case you didn't know, is white, like all other Indian agents I know of. His siding with the mine owners—what the Choctaws will see as siding with whites against Indians—is bound to stir up even more discontent, which will lead—inevitably, in my opinion—to even more trouble in the coal fields."

"I have to agree with you."

Jessie beckoned to the waiter, who brought their check. "I'll pay this," she told Ki, who had still not finished his meal. "I'll see you when I get back from visiting Arthur Pryor."

"Good luck."

"Thanks. I have a feeling I'm going to need the lion's share of that commodity if I'm to get anywhere with Pryor."

Jessie had been waiting in Arthur Pryor's outer office for nearly an hour when the man's receptionist announced, "Mr. Pryor will see you now."

Jessie rose and entered the office to find a thin-as-a-rail man with gold-rimmed spectacles seated behind a rosewood desk.

"Mr. Pryor," Jessie greeted him and held out her hand.

He looked up, took her hand in his limp one, gave it a perfunctory shake, and said, "Please have a seat, Miss Starbuck. What can I do for you?"

"I've come to see you," Jessie said as she sat down across the desk from the Indian agent, "to discuss the agreement you made yesterday with Messrs. Carruthers and Fanshaw."

Pryor said nothing as the sunlight streaming through the window glinted on the lenses of his spectacles, to give him a faintly sinister look.

Jessie decided to take the bull by the horns. "I think it was an unwise agreement, Mr. Pryor."

"Really, Miss Starbuck?" Pryor took off his glasses. He removed a white linen handkerchief from a pocket and proceeded to polish them as he squinted at Jessie through obviously nearsighted eyes. "In what respect? Or respects?" He replaced his glasses.

"It's too one-sided, Mr. Pryor. It gives everything to the mine owners and nothing to the Indians you represent."

"It furthers commerce, Miss Starbuck. Important commerce that benefits the individual mine owners—and I know you are one of that select group—and it deprives the Indians of nothing."

"Nothing except an opportunity to express their opinions about how the coal in Choctaw Nation is to be used and by whom."

"I am not running a public forum here. I am running an office that ministers to the needs of the government's wards."

Jessie felt the flesh of her face growing warm, and she was certain she was flushing as conflicting feelings stirred within her. As calmly as she could manage, she continued, "I wonder if it would not have been better, Mr. Pryor, to wait before considering the implementation of such a sweeping agreement that gives mine owners like myself the right to do anything and everything to expand their operations."

"Everything within reason," Pryor said coldly. And then, arching an eyebrow, "You hardly talk like the owner of one of the republic's lucrative mines, Miss Starbuck."

Jessie decided to ignore the thrust. "You probably know that yesterday some Choctaws attacked the workers at the mine I lease to Mr. Luke Hodges."

"I have heard of that unfortunate incident."

"Then you no doubt know that it was an expression of anger at the way the coal is being mined here and by whom it is being mined. It was an attempt to drive out Mr. Hodges and the men he employs. I submit to you that I think it will not be the last such attempt, especially in light of the fact that your agreement with Messrs. Carruthers and Fanshaw is sure to stoke into angry life fires that are already burning and threatening to destroy the peace and order of the republic."

"That is a rather melodramatic interpretation of a single, though admittedly rowdy, event."

"I do not agree, Mr. Pryor. I think it is the first scuffle in what may soon become a dangerous battle between the Choctaws and the people engaged in mining coal on their tribal lands. It is for this reason that I am asking you to rescind your agreement—for now at least."

"Miss Starbuck, I have served as Choctaw agent for nearly four years now, as you probably know. In the early years of my tenure in this position, the coal that you and others are now mining lay in the ground untouched by anyone. It was not until you and others like you made arrangements with Chief Bryant to exploit those valuable mineral deposits that the Choctaws benefited from an asset that had heretofore lain absolutely worthless under their very noses, so to speak.

"They did not mine that coal. They ignored it. Later on, they were glad to sign agreements with people like yourself, since it meant that their tribal treasury would be fattened by the royalties paid to it, again by people like yourself. Now voices of discontent are being heard in the land. Voices that are calling for Indian ownership of the mines and for the expulsion of the miners from the republic, as intruders who have no right to be where they are or to do what they have been so successfully doing now for some time. Miss Starbuck, as I'm sure you know, the Indians are an unsophisticated people. They are like children in many ways, and I do not say that to denigrate them. Children can be delightful as we all know. But they can also be greedy, as witness the movement now afoot among the Choctaws to take over the mines, run them themselves, and reap *all* the monetary rewards such a change would bring them.

"That, I say, is an effort that is doomed to fail. The Choctaws are not capable of managing such complex enterprises. They would soon ruin the mines, and then no one, least of all

100

them, would benefit. It is for these reasons that I signed that agreement which has brought you here this morning. I did it for the good of all concerned—the Choctaws, the mine owners, the miners employed in the mines, and the general economy of the region. I trust you will try to see my motives and understand them, Miss Starbuck, rather than make me, as you seem to be trying to do, the villain of this piece."

"Then I take it you will not consider rescinding—even temporarily—the agreement?"

"Your assumption is quite correct."

Jessie rose. "I'm very sorry to hear that, Mr. Pryor. I hope you won't have occasion to be sorry that you would not change your mind."

Pryor stared up at her. "It was good of you to call, Miss Starbuck." The sunlight glinted again on the lenses of his glasses as he added, "It is always a pleasure to meet with people like yourself who have, as do I, the best interests of the Choctaw people at heart."

Jessie left the Indian agent's office wondering if she had heard him correctly. *He* had the best interests of the Choctaw people at heart? Did he really believe that? If he did, she was convinced that he was deluding himself, at least in the specific matter of the agreement he had signed the day before with Monty Carruthers and Leonard Fanshaw.

★

Chapter 7

As she walked through the streets of McAlester, Jessie decided to make one more attempt to persuade Monty Carruthers to set aside the agreement he had made the day before with Arthur Pryor. She was convinced that if Carruthers went ahead with his and Fanshaw's plans to develop the new coal deposits and build a spur line from the main track of the Katy railroad to the new mine, there would be trouble. Trouble that could, she was convinced, be avoided by the simple expedient of doing nothing for the time being.

She retraced her steps, turned a corner, and headed down the street toward Carruthers's office.

"Oh, it's you, Miss Starbuck," said Carruthers's receptionist, recognizing Jessie as she entered the office and closed the door behind her. "Have you seen him perhaps?"

"Seen who?"

"Mr. Carruthers."

"No, I haven't. I came by to speak to him. Isn't he here?"

The receptionist shook her head and began to bite her lower lip as she looked from Jessie to the empty office visible through the open door behind her.

"When do you expect him to return?" Jessie asked.

The receptionist turned back to face her and let out a plaintive wail. Then her hands shot up to cover her mouth, and only muffled sobs could be heard through her clenched fingers.

Jessie went to her and put an arm around her shoulders. "What is it? What's wrong? Has something happened to Mr. Carruthers?"

"That's just it, I don't *know*!"

"Come over here and sit down," Jessie said, leading the woman across the room to a number of chairs lining one wall. She helped the woman sit down and then took a seat next to her.

"Now, tell me why you're so upset."

"Well, maybe I shouldn't be upset," the receptionist said as if she were talking to herself. "One cannot expect a person to adhere to the same routine every single working day of his life, can one?"

Jessie did not respond to what she recognized as a rhetorical question. Instead, she reached out and took one of the receptionist's hands in her own and gently stroked it, trying to calm the woman, who was, she was sure, close to hysteria.

"I came to work this morning as usual. But to my surprise, the front door was locked. I had to use my own key to admit myself. That was the first unusual thing I noticed. You see, Mr. Carruthers invariably arrives at the office before I do."

As the receptionist sniffled and dabbed at her eyes with a lace handkerchief she had taken from a pocket in her tailored white blouse, Jessie said, "Please go on."

The receptionist gave her a dazed look. Then, recovering herself, she continued, "Well, when I came inside, Mr. Carruthers was not in his office. I thought that strange and I began at once to worry. But then I decided Mr. Carruthers had been delayed. Or perhaps he had decided not to come to the office today and would send me word to that effect.

"I told myself I would not let myself be upset over nothing. So I went about my business just as if everything was perfectly normal, but of course, everything was not the least bit normal."

"Did Mr. Carruthers arrive later?"

"No!" The word was a cry, an exclamation of alarm. It seemed to echo in the still, dry air of the room. "I haven't seen him at all. I sent a messenger to the mine to see if he was there, but the man returned to say that Mr. Carruthers had not put in an appearance at the mine. No one there had seen him.

"Well, when I heard that, you can imagine I was close to becoming distraught. I didn't though. I got a good firm grip on my nerves, telling myself that Mr. Carruthers would expect me to carry on as usual in his unexpected absence—"

As the receptionist buried her face in her hands and began to weep, Jessie patted her shoulder and murmured words of encouragement.

The woman raised her head. She dabbed at the tears coursing down her cheeks. "I then sent the messenger to Mr. Carruthers's home to see if he was there. But his housekeeper reported that he had not been present at his home when she arrived at the house at eight o'clock this morning."

"Perhaps he had some business to take care of out of town. Business that he either forgot or chose not to mention to you."

An annoyed expression flitted across the receptionist's face. "Mr. Carruthers always keeps me informed of his plans and daily agenda. He would have told me if he had intended to be out of town or if something unusual required him to absent himself from the office.

"No, I am convinced that something has happened to him. Something too terrible to contemplate perhaps. There has been trouble at the mine of late as you may know. The miners are threatening to go on strike. There has also been the recent series of difficulties with the Indians about Mr. Carruthers's business enterprises. Miss Starbuck, I have to say it. I suspect *foul play!*"

"You must get hold of yourself," Jessie said. "It's only been a relatively short time Mr. Carruthers has not been seen, so far as we know. Yesterday—everything was as usual then?"

The receptionist nodded. "I wish there was something I could do. It is awful not knowing what has happened to him and not knowing what to do."

"I'll make inquiries concerning Mr. Carruthers's whereabouts," Jessie volunteered, causing a hopeful look to flood the receptionist's face.

"But I've already done that," the woman pointed out a moment later, her hopeful look fading fast. "I sent a messenger—"

"Yes, I know," Jessie interrupted. "But I had in mind making inquiries in other places." Before the receptionist could question her as she appeared to be about to do, Jessie rose. "I'll report back to you later on if I find out anything."

"Oh, thank you ever so much, Miss Starbuck. I shall be looking forward to hearing from you."

Once outside the office, Jessie headed directly for the hotel. She was relieved upon arriving at her destination to find Ki seated in the lobby and reading the local newspaper.

"How did it go?" he asked her as she joined him.

"Badly. Pryor wouldn't consider canceling or even temporarily withdrawing the agreement he made with Carruthers and Fanshaw."

"Then you've struck a stone wall, looks like."

"Ki, I went to Monty Carruthers's office on the way back here. I had the idea that I might be able to persuade him to change his mind and not rush into developing his new mine. When I got to his office, I found out from his receptionist that he seems to have disappeared."

"Disappeared?"

"Well, that may be too strong a word to use. But he didn't show up at his office as usual this morning, and his receptionist told me that was most unusual and that he had not told her he would not be in. She is very worried, and I think she may have reason to be if it's true, as she claims, that Carruthers is a man of rather fixed habits."

"Even men of fixed habits sometimes encounter the unexpected and have to change their plans without having the opportunity to advise anyone of the change in advance."

"You're right, of course. But what if his plans were changed for him? By someone or several someones who meant him harm?"

Ki put down his newspaper and stared at Jessie. "What do you think has happened to him—if indeed anything has?"

"I don't know. But he told me that Chief Bryant was apparently very upset about the agreement signed by Arthur Pryor. If Daniel Marshal found out about that agreement, he, too, would be made rather unhappy by it, I'll bet. One or both of them might have decided to do something drastic about it."

"Like kidnapping Carruthers to prevent him from pursuing his plans?"

"It's a possibility, you've got to admit."

"So is the chance that Carruthers simply decided to take an unannounced vacation."

"I wonder . . . ," Jessie began and then fell silent.

"Tell me."

"I wonder if Leonard Fanshaw is going about his business as usual this morning."

"I see what you're getting at."

"If he has also suddenly disappeared, we might safely conclude that something ugly is afoot. However, if he has not, then we might conclude that Carruthers's disappearance is not ominous, since if someone like Daniel Marshal or Chief Bryant wanted to act to stop those two men they would probably have acted against both of them simultaneously."

"Not necessarily, Jessie. Maybe if someone has made off with Carruthers for some nefarious purpose, they feel whatever they do to him will serve as sufficient warning for Fanshaw and others like them—including yourself, by the way."

"I'm going to see if I can locate Fanshaw."

As Jessie headed at a brisk pace for the door, Ki rose and called out, "Wait for me."

She did, and when he caught up with her, they left the hotel and made their way through the crowds in the streets to the office of Leonard Fanshaw.

"Is Mr. Fanshaw in?" Jessie asked the eyeshaded clerk inside the well-appointed office.

"I'm sorry, he's not. May I be of some service?"

"When do you expect him?" Jessie asked.

The clerk pulled a Waltham watch from the pocket of his vest, snapped it open, peered at it, and declared, "Actually he should have returned here over an hour ago."

"Where would he have been coming from?" Ki asked.

"He was to meet with the railroad's freight manager, Mr. Francis Anders, at eight A.M. this morning, and then he had a meeting with Mr. James Connaught of the McAlester Lumber Company at nine, about the purchase of some track timber to be used for ties on the new spur line. Then he was to return here. Was he expecting you?"

"No," Jessie replied, "but it is rather important that I see him. I'm Jessica Starbuck. I've known Mr. Fanshaw for some time—"

"He has mentioned you several times in my presence, Miss Starbuck," the clerk said with what sounded like an obsequious simper to Jessie. "Always in the most respectful terms, of course. Would you care to wait for Mr. Fanshaw to return?"

Jessie shook her head. "Thank you for your time and the information you've given us."

"Good day," the clerk said as Jessie, with Ki at her side, left the office and returned to the street.

"Let's pay a call on the local lumber company," she said. "I want to see if Fanshaw was there this morning."

They found the lumber yard a noisy and dusty place where it took them some time to track down James Connaught, the owner of the business, in the labyrinthine corridors formed by tall stacks of raw lumber that towered above their heads. When they finally came upon him, he was marking some raw white pine with a red crayon, and he didn't look up when Jessie introduced herself. Nor did he speak.

"Has Mr. Fanshaw visited you this morning?" she asked him, getting right to the heart of the matter that concerned her.

"Who wants to know?"

"I'm Jessica Starbuck and this gentlemen is a friend of mine. We're business associates of Mr. Fanshaw's," she said, telling a white lie for not the first time in her life.

"Leonard never showed up here this morning as planned. That's not like him. But maybe he found another supplier somewhere. Everybody tries to underbid everybody else in the lumber business. All of us want the railroad's business. It eats up lumber for ties like a desert soaks up rain."

"We understand," Ki said, "that Mr. Fanshaw had an appointment with you at nine o'clock this morning."

"He did, but like I said, he never kept it. Which, as I also said, is not like Leonard, not like him a'tall. Are you two in the market for some lumber?"

107

"No, we're not," Jessie answered. "Thank you for talking to us."

They retraced their steps through the maze of stacked lumber, the sound of saws making conversation impossible.

Once out on the street again, Ki glanced at Jessie and said, "Now we're going to pay a call on Mr. Francis Anders, am I right?"

"You are."

They found Francis Anders in a small room—a mere cubbyhole of a room in the depot—that served him as an office.

"Yes, indeed," he replied in response to Jessie's question. "Mr. Fanshaw was here at eight o'clock right on the dot. Punctual as usual, he was."

"What time did he leave here?"

"Fifteen to nine. Thereabouts. Why do you ask?"

"We're trying to locate Mr. Fanshaw, and we're checking with the people he was scheduled to see this morning, yourself among them," Jessie explained.

"You'd do better, mayhap, to see him in his office. He does have an office in town. It's located at—"

"Thank you," Jessie said. "Thank you very much."

They left Anders poring over his bills of lading, wetting the stub of a pencil on his tongue as he did so and then making cryptic notes on the many documents littering his desk.

"Fanshaw could have had a change of plans," Ki offered as they left the depot.

"Or someone could have changed his plans for him."

"What now?"

"I think I should pay a visit to Chief Bryant. I'd like to see what he has to say about the apparent disappearance of a man he had angry words with recently."

"Jessie, hold on a moment. You're not sure Fanshaw has disappeared. You're not sure that Monty Carruthers has either, for that matter."

"I admit that. But I think their absence from the places they are supposed to be is definitely suspicious. I also think it's not likely that both men would suddenly and without explanation disrupt their normal schedules. Ki, I want you to do something for me, if you will."

"What is it?"

"In the interest of saving time, I'd like you to try to locate Daniel Marshal and ask him if he knows anything about the present whereabouts of either Fanshaw or Carruthers. While you're doing that, I'll call on Chief Bryant. We can meet back at the hotel once we've talked to both men—if we can locate them."

"I'm on my way."

When Ki had gone, Jessie strode down the street on her way to Chief Bryant's home, which was located just outside the town limits.

When she got to it, she found the doors closed and the shades drawn on all the windows. She knocked on the door but received no answer. She was about to leave and return to town when three Choctaw men on horseback rode by in the near distance.

Jessie hailed them, and they halted, watching her approach.

"I'm Jessie Starbuck," she said when she reached them.

"We know you," one of the men said. "You mine our coal."

Jessie hesitated, momentarily taken aback by the aggressive statement. "Do you know where I might find Chief Bryant?"

None of them answered her at first. They exchanged glances, and then the one who had already spoken said, "What do you want with our chief?"

None of your business, Jessie thought, but she said, "The chief and I are business acquaintances. I came to talk to him, but it appears he is not at home."

"It is a good thing for him that he is not at home," the same man said sullenly.

"I beg your pardon?"

"As well you might. You and others like you have stolen our coal. If Chief Bryant were at home, you would no doubt steal from him anything of value he may possess."

"You don't even know me and you dare to insult me like that!" Jessie said, her temper steaming. "I'll have you know that I have never stolen anything from anyone—"

"Maybe we should take her too, Colin," one of the other two Choctaw riders said. "Give her a taste of the same medicine. Chief Bryant would like that, I am thinking."

The men were silent then and so was Jessie, who felt a sudden chill at the ominously spoken words. What was it they

109

were talking about? She took a step backward, prepared to run, wondering at the same time if she were being foolish.

"Take her!" ordered Colin.

Before Jessie could turn and flee from them, the other two men were out of their saddles and taking hold of her arms. She struggled to free herself, but she could barely move.

"One of you," Colin directed, "put her aboard your horse and bring her with us."

The two men holding Jessie captive began to drag her over to where they had left their horses. She twisted and turned, trying to break free of them, unable for the moment to think of what fate might be awaiting her at their hands, intent only on freeing herself and getting safely away.

They were about to place her aboard a dapple when she saw her chance and seized it. She kicked out as the two men started to lift her, and her right foot slammed into the groin of the man on her left. He instantly let go of her, doubled over, and clutched his genitals, uttering a howl of agony as he did so.

Jessie fisted her free hand and rammed it into the face of the other man. She thought she heard bone crack. Then, as blood began to flow from the man's nose, she hit him again before he could recover from the shock of her unexpected attack, and he lost his grip on her.

She ran.

With arms and legs pumping and her breath coming in harsh gulps, she ran back the way she had come, desperate to reach town before these three men could outride her and once again take her captive.

She heard them coming after her moments later. The sound of their horses' hooves pounding the ground was a thick thunder in the country air. She glanced over her shoulder without slowing her pace and saw them closing in on her. A strangled cry escaped from her throat as she fled from them. Her arms flailed in the air as if she were trying to swim swiftly through it. Her hair flew out behind her. With her lungs bursting, she swerved to the left and ran into a thick grove of sycamores, among which were many saplings. She was almost sure that her pursuers would not be able to follow her into the grove.

She was right. They could not follow her into the dense forest—on horseback. But the two men with Colin leaped from their saddles and ran on foot into the woods.

"Give up!" one of them yelled. "You'll never get away from us."

But Jessie wouldn't give up—not until the last breath she would ever take had left her body. She ran on, crying out in pain at one point when strands of her hair caught in a sapling's low-slung branches and were ripped from her scalp. But she didn't slow down. Not for a minute.

She heard cursing behind her. She heard one of the men fall. She heard them both continue pursuit of her. They came crashing through the trees like unseen beasts determined to run her to ground. When they did—

She wouldn't let herself think of that.

Light. Up ahead. Where the woods thinned out and open land stretched beyond them.

She emerged from the woods a moment later, and her heart froze at the sight of Colin standing directly in front of her, his horse ground-hitched nearby. Her momentum propelled her forward, and she collided with him. As she felt his arms close around her, she realized that he had ridden around the woods in the hope of doing what he had just done—capturing her as she emerged from them.

Too weak from her exertions to fight, she let herself be practically thrown aboard Colin's horse and then rode behind him after he had swung into the saddle and moved out.

Ki, not knowing where to find Daniel Marshal but knowing that a town's best source of information was the livery barn, made his way to the one located in the center of McAlester. There he found a number of men of various ages seated outside the door of the livery on cracker barrels and assorted boxes as they sunned themselves and gossiped.

"Good day to you," he greeted them.

Mumbled greetings were uttered around the chaws most of the men had tucked in their cheeks.

"I'm looking for a fellow," Ki told them. "His name's Daniel Marshal. Any of you boys know where I can find him?"

A man whittling busily said to the man next to him, without bothering to look up from his work, "When somebody's looking for somebody else, chances are good that the somebody doing the looking's either the law or somebody out to settle a grudge against the somebody they're looking for."

"Uh-yup," was the laconic response from the whittler's companion.

"Wouldn't want to cause somebody like Danny no trouble." the whittler said. "Might, though, if you told tales about him to strangers."

"I reckon you're about right," the whittler's companion remarked, neither of them looking at Ki but their remarks obviously addressed to him.

"I'm not the law," he assured them. "I'm a friend of Danny's who just got into town the other day and hasn't had a chance to look him up until now. I've got an important message for him. It has to do with the moves the mine owners are fixing to make against him and those who think the same way he does about the exploitation of the Choctaw coal deposits."

Ki waited for lightning to strike him for his blatant lies, but the sky overhead remained clear.

The men in front of the livery, every last one of them, were looking at him now. He waited, hoping.

The whittler came through for him after a long, thoughtful silence. "Might be that Danny's hard at work like usual over at his shack he uses to organize the actions him and some others are fixing to take against the intruders."

Ki was sure that the reference to "intruders" meant mine owners like Jessie. "Where would this shack of his be located?" he inquired.

When he had been given directions to it, he thanked the men and made his way through the streets to the far side of town. The shack, he discovered when he reached it, was exactly that—a shack built of raw lumber that was full of knotholes and that had a tar-papered roof set at a slant so the rain would readily run off it. There was an open padlock on the door, which could be covered by a piece of rawhide—as if that would fool anyone into thinking that there was no lock beneath it, to be picked or shot off its hinges.

Ki didn't bother to knock. He opened the door, which hung haphazardly on leather hinges, and stepped inside. The interior of the structure was gloomy despite the fact that a coal oil lamp burnt on a table. Its smoky globe, which obviously had not been cleaned in a long time, let little light through it.

Marshal, who was seated at a rickety table writing with a quill pen in a ledger, looked up as Ki entered and, when he saw who his visitor was, stiffened.

"What do you want?"

"To talk to you, Marshal."

"I've got nothing to say to you or to your friend, Miss Starbuck, that I didn't say when we first met on the street the other day."

"Where are they, Marshal?"

Ki's question was met with a blank expression. But Ki had seen the flicker of Marshal's eyes, a kind of tic that revealed the man's nervousness.

"You deaf, Marshal?"

"I don't know who or what you're talking about."

"Is that a fact now? Wait! Don't tell me it is, because I happen to believe it isn't." Ki looked around the dingy room. "So this is where you do your deviltry."

Marshal remained silent as he pushed his chair back from his desk.

He's getting ready for action, Ki thought. "What did you do with Leonard Fanshaw and Monty Carruthers?"

"Get the hell out of here!"

Ki made his move. He sprang forward, placed his left hand flat on the surface of Marshal's desk, and vaulted over it to land beside the man. He yanked Marshal to his feet and threw him against the rear wall of the shack. He moved closer to the man and got a grip on his shirt. Thrusting his fisted hand upward, he tilted Marshal's head backward until its crown was pressed against the wall.

Marshal used both hands to try to break Ki's grip, but he failed to do so. "Damn you, you've got no right—"

"Let's talk about rights since you brought the subject up," Ki said icily. "What about the rights of Carruthers and Fanshaw? Don't they have the right to be free of plots hatched by the likes of you?"

"I told you. I don't know what the hell you're talking about."

"Come on, Marshal, don't treat me like a fool, because I'm not one. You kidnapped them, didn't you? Where've you got them? Or have you killed them?"

113

Marshal groaned as Ki pressed his fist against his throat in a successful effort to temporarily cut off the man's air supply. A moment later, Ki reduced the pressure. "I asked after you at the livery, Marshal. They weren't inclined, the livery barn bums down there, to say much until I told them a lie or two like I was your best bosom buddy. Then they opened up and one of them said maybe more than he ought to have. Like this is the place where you plan what actions you and those on your side intend to take against the mine owners to run them out of the republic. I figure you plotted—probably right here—to make Carruthers and Fanshaw disappear."

When Marshal said nothing, Ki pressed hard against the man's windpipe. Marshal gagged. Ki pressed harder. Marshal's eyes bulged.

"You've got a choice," Ki told him. "Tell me what I want to know or choke to death."

The skin of Marshal's face turned red, then a pale blue. The blue deepened as he continued to gag and struggle, with decreasing strength, and in vain, to free himself.

"You want to talk to me?" Ki asked.

Marshal's eyes widened.

"Blink once for 'yes.'"

Marshal blinked once.

Ki let him go and remained directly in front of him as he rubbed his throat with both hands and noisily sucked air into his lungs.

"What have you done with them? Are they alive? Dead?"

Marshal shook his head.

"I'd better ask one question at a time. Are they alive?"

Marshal nodded. Then, in a raspy voice, said, "As far as I know, yes."

Ki raised his hands as if to reach for Marshal's throat.

"I took them both. First, Carruthers. Then, Fanshaw."

"What did you do with them?"

"Turned them over—" Marshal began to cough and then to gag again.

Ki waited for him to recover.

When he had, he continued, "Turned them—Chief Bryant."

114

"You turned them over to Chief Bryant?" When Marshal nodded, Ki asked, "Why?"

"To be punished. The chief refused Carruthers permission to develop new coal deposits he claims he's found and also refused Fanshaw permission to build a spur line out to those deposits. But they were going to go ahead anyway. Bryant intended to stop them."

"How?" Ki was afraid of the answer he might get, but the question had to be asked.

Marshal answered it.

"Where?" Ki barked.

"At the old tribal council ground."

"Where's that?"

Marshal told him.

"You're going to take me there," Ki muttered. "Let's go." He seized Marshal by the shoulder and practically dragged him out of the shack.

As they continued their journey, Jessie and the three Choctaw riders passed numerous people walking and riding horses or in wagons, all of them heading in the same direction.

After a ride that lasted nearly twenty minutes, the four arrived in a clearing surrounded by tall post oaks. The man behind whom Jessie had been riding ordered her to dismount. She did so by the simple expedient of sliding down over the rump and tail of the man's horse.

She had intended to try to make a run for it, hoping to lose herself in the crowd of Choctaws gathered in the clearing, but the other two men who had been riding with her quickly dismounted and, taking her by the arms, led her through the crowd to the center of the clearing, where Chief Bryant was standing with his arms folded across his chest. He showed no sign of surprise at the sight of her, but he did turn a questioning glance in the direction of the Choctaw named Colin, who came up to stand beside Jessie and the two men holding her captive.

"She was at your house when we passed by," Colin explained. "We thought we'd bring her here and make a three-party affair out of the matter."

"Chief Bryant," Jessie began, "I want to talk to you."

"There is nothing to say," the chief said sharply. To the three Choctaws, he said, "Hold her while we deal with the other two."

Bryant gave a signal, and a man went running from the crowd into the woods. He emerged a few minutes later with four other men he had evidently summoned. Two held Leonard Fanshaw prisoner between them; two firmly gripped a vociferously protesting Carruthers.

Jessie was not entirely surprised to see them. On the trip to this spot, she had begun to suspect—based on the remark one of the Choctaws had made to Colin about making something or other a "three-party affair"—that she was about to join the inexplicably vanished Carruthers and Fanshaw for whatever Fate—and the Choctaws—had in store for the three of them.

"We came here today to see justice done," Chief Bryant intoned as the four men led their prisoners to two stout oaks and began to tie them to the trees, which towered above the crowd. "Choctaw tribal justice," the chief added. "You all know that our ancestors decreed the kind of punishment that must be meted out to anyone who has tried to harm the Choctaw people. Those two," he pointed at Fanshaw and Carruthers, who were now securely bound to the two oak trees, their chests and faces pressed against them, their arms encircling them and tied tightly at the wrists, "those two, by their actions, have injured the tribe and all who are a part of it. They steal from us and call it business. They must be taught a lesson, and it is for that reason that they have been brought here today with the help of our brother in blood, Daniel Marshal."

A cheer went up from the crowd at Bryant's mention of the name.

"Chief Bryant—" Jessie said, trying but failing to twist free of the men who were holding her so firmly.

"Silence!" he demanded and then said to the crowd, "This woman is one of those who has injured us. She, too, will pay her debt to us today. But first—the men." Bryant gestured.

Two men emerged from the crowd. In their hands were black leather bullwhips. They walked over to where the other four men were in the process of ripping Carruthers's and

116

Fanshaw's shirts to bare their backs.

"You've got no right to do this, dammit!" Carruthers bellowed.

"Let us go!" Fanshaw cried. "We'll pay you—"

"Silence!" Bryant again thundered. Then, to the men with the whips, he said, "Proceed."

The men raised their arms as they stood some distance behind Carruthers and Fanshaw. They braced themselves, swung, and struck.

Jessie winced as both bullwhips slashed across the bare backs of the prisoners.

Fanshaw screamed. Carruthers remained grimly silent.

The whips rose and slithered through the air like two giant black snakes. They landed.

A cry, more of a collective moan, went up from the people in the crowd as they avidly watched the proceedings.

Jessie found herself counting while not wanting to. Three, four, five . . .

The faces of the men with the whips were expressionless as they continued their grim work. Their whips rose in the air, whirled, and descended to land with flat slapping sounds on flesh.

Fanshaw was no longer screaming. Now he was whimpering.

Tied to the tree on his left, Carruthers had made no single sound—yet. But as the whip in the hands of the man standing behind him, with his legs planted far apart, struck again and yet again, he could apparently stand it no longer. As blood appeared like thin red furrows where the whips had most recently cut into the flesh of his back, he threw back his head and howled in agony.

Jessie wanted to put her hands over her ears to stop the awful sound. It invaded her mind and played havoc with her thoughts. "Chief Bryant!" she heard herself cry in a loud voice. "Stop this!"

He ignored her.

The whipping continued.

She looked away, biting her lower lip. Soon, she knew, it would be her turn. Could she endure what awaited her?

"Enough!" Bryant called out, holding up a restraining hand.

The two men with the whips stepped back and lowered their whips.

"Untie them!" Bryant ordered, and the four men who had brought Carruthers and Fanshaw to this place of primitive tribal punishment did so.

As both men slumped to the ground, their heads hanging down, Bryant slowly turned until he was facing Jessie. "Now it is your turn," he said solemnly.

"Chief, this is not the way to settle our dispute," Jessie argued. "Whipping people won't—"

"We want justice," Bryant said, interrupting her. "We will get justice. One way or another, we will. What is happening here today is meant as a warning to you three and to all others like you, who will suffer the same or a worse fate if they persist in inflicting injury upon the Choctaw people." Bryant gestured peremptorily.

The two men holding her prisoner forced Jessie to walk with them to the tree to which Carruthers had been bound. One of the pair cruelly booted Carruthers away from the base of the tree, and then both men quickly tied Jessie to his place.

"Ten stripes!" Bryant ordered.

One of the men who had helped to administer the chief's decreed punishment to Fanshaw and Carruthers stepped forward and raised his whip.

Jessie, who could not see him, had heard his footsteps, had heard the sudden anticipatory silence that had descended upon the watching crowd. She braced herself.

She heard the whip whine its ugly way through the air before she felt it land on her back. She gritted her teeth to keep from crying out as the whip was withdrawn. Her back burned as if someone had touched a flaming brand to it.

The next time the whip lashed her it sent white lights flashing wildly in front of her eyes. Her head jerked violently backward and then forward, her forehead striking the trunk of the tree.

Before the lash could land again, she heard the shouted word "*Stop!*" Relief flooded her, dousing the white lights and bringing her world back into focus once again.

She strained to but could not see Ki, whose voice she had just recognized. She did hear the next words he spoke.

"If any of you makes a move, I'll cut Marshal's throat." A pause. "Untie her."

Jessie managed to remain standing once she had been freed, despite an almost overwhelming weakness in her knees. She turned, one hand outstretched to touch the tree for support, and saw Ki standing beside a fringe-topped surrey in the distance. He was holding Daniel Marshal in front of him, one of the man's arms twisted behind his back. In Ki's right hand was one of his metal throwing stars. The tip of one of the *shuriken*'s five sharp blades was pressed against the artery on the side of Marshal's neck, pressed so hard that it made a deep indentation in the flesh of his neck.

"What is the meaning of this, Daniel?" Chief Bryant bellowed.

"He wants the whites," Marshal replied. "He says he'll kill me if you don't turn them over to him."

"Who is he?"

"Never mind who I am," Ki shouted. "Help those two men over there. Jessie, can you walk?"

"Yes," she called back and started for the surrey, hoping her legs wouldn't give out on her.

"Get in," Ki told her when she reached the surrey. "In the back." As Jessie climbed into the rear seat, several Choctaw men, supporting Carruthers and Fanshaw, arrived. "In the back," Ki told the Indians and waited while they helped the two men to climb in beside Jessie. Then he forced Marshal into the front seat, climbed in next to him, and ordered him to drive the team.

As Marshal obeyed, moving the team of matched grays out, Ki yelled over his shoulder, "Don't any of you folks follow us. If you do, your fair-haired boy here will die. That's a promise, and you can bet your boots I'll keep it."

Chief Bryant and the other Choctaws watched in silence as Marshal set the grays to galloping and the surrey careened away from the clearing.

★

Chapter 8

"Where did you come from?" Jessie asked Ki when the Choc-taws had been left far behind them in the clearing.

"I found out from Marshal where Carruthers and Bryant were," he replied. "I figured instead of going back to the hotel to meet you as we'd planned, I'd have Marshal take me to where the whipping he'd told me about was scheduled to take place. I'd hoped to prevent it, but I got there too late. I certainly never expected to see you there, Jessie. How—"

"I was at Chief Bryant's house when three Choctaw men rode by on their way to the whipping. I hailed them, which turned out to be a mistake. They wound up taking me out there to suffer the same fate as Monty and Leonard did."

"I'm glad I got there before they'd gone too far in your case," Ki said.

"So am I, believe me." Jessie turned her attention to the two men sharing the back seat of the surrey with her. "Are you all right now?" she asked them.

"I feel like I've been skinned alive," Fanshaw murmured, his voice weak.

"The bastards!" Carruthers muttered. "Excuse me, Jessie. That was out of line."

"I understand how you feel, Monty," Jessie assured him.

"I feel like going home and getting a gun and going back there and blowing those Indians into kingdom come!" Carruthers declared hotly.

"There's a lot more of them than there are of you," Ki pointed out.

"Maybe I'll start with that one," Carruthers said, his angry eyes on Marshal in the front seat.

"Anytime you want to try to take me, Carruthers," Marshal said with surprising calm under the circumstances, "you just let me know and I'll oblige you."

"I thought you and Chief Bryant didn't exactly see eye-to-eye," Jessie said to Marshal.

"We didn't and we still don't. But the chief came to me and said he thought it was time we joined forces against the likes of you. He said there was more strength in union than in division, and I had to admit the old boy was right."

"So you kidnapped Monty and me," an indignant Fanshaw accused.

"I did. And I'll do it again—or whatever else it takes to get rid of you."

"Not if we take care of you first," Carruthers spat.

Marshal, as he drove and the surrey rocked from side to side on the rutted road which led to town, dismissed the mine owner's threat with a shrug.

"You think I wouldn't make a move on you?" Carruthers asked angrily. "You think I don't know how to fight fire with fire, is that it?"

"You didn't put up much of a fight when I took you right off the streets of McAlester and turned you over to Chief Bryant's men," Marshal taunted.

Carruthers spluttered wordlessly for a moment and then managed to mutter, "You took me by surprise that time. Next time—You won't sneak up on me again, I can tell you that. I'll be ready for you next time. With a gun!"

"Bluster and balderdash," Marshal mocked, grinning from ear to ear. "I doubt you could hit the side of a barn if you fired a gun at it."

121

There was a moment of utter silence, and then Carruthers gave a shriek of rage and sprang forward. His reaching hands went around Marshal's neck, jerking the man backward. As Marshal lost control of the team, the surrey swerved to the right and then to the left.

Ki turned in his seat and threw a fist that caught Carruthers on the jaw, snapping his head backward. He had to hit the man a second time before Carruthers would let go of Marshal. Then, as Marshal bent forward, coughing and choking, his hands around his neck, which bore the red imprints of his attacker's fingers, Ki grabbed the reins and, after several minutes of tense struggle, managed to bring the team under control. He slowed the two grays and then brought them to a halt. They stood shaking their heads and snorting.

"Get out!" he barked and gave Marshal a shove that sent him tumbling out of the surrey.

"You can walk the rest of the way back to town," Ki told him as Marshal stood on the side of the road glaring at him and Carruthers.

Ki slapped the rumps of the team with the reins and moved them out. Within seconds, Marshal was left far behind, and then he disappeared from sight as the surrey rounded a bend on only three wheels.

"Slow down, Ki," Jessie said. "We almost turned over back there."

Ki slowed the team, getting them and his own temper under control once again.

"You shouldn't have done that, Monty," Fanshaw said meekly, not quite meeting the mine owner's eyes. "You've really made an enemy for life out of Marshal now by attacking him the way you did."

"What should I have done? Begged his pardon for escaping from those savages back there?"

"Now don't get riled, Monty," Fanshaw said. "I just thought I ought to speak my mind. I have an interest in all this too, you know, and I'd far rather have friends than enemies as we negotiate the shoals and rapids of the dangerous course we're following."

Carruthers swore under his breath while simultaneously giving Fanshaw a look of complete contempt.

"We could offer Marshal a small stipend if he will let us be," Fanshaw suggested, his voice low, his eyes shifty.

"Stipend?" Carruthers roared. "I wouldn't give that man the time of day, never mind money."

"Gentlemen," Jessie said, "calm down. Fighting among ourselves isn't going to get us anywhere."

"You told Marshal back there," Ki said, addressing Carruthers, "that you intended to start toting a gun. I think that's a wise move, given the present climate and circumstances you're facing. Fanshaw, you ought to give some thought to doing the selfsame thing."

"I've never fired a gun, not in all my born days," an obviously shocked Fanshaw declared in a tone of disbelief that suggested Ki had just asked him to fly to the moon.

"Just a suggestion," Ki said mildly.

"I happen to think it's a good one," Jessie offered. "I for one intend to go about armed from now on."

Both Fanshaw and Carruthers stared at her as if she had just announced the imminent advent of Armageddon.

No one spoke during the next few minutes, as the surrey wound its way through the coal fields to McAlester.

But everyone spoke at once and excitedly some time later as an underground coal mine that bordered the road they were traveling exploded, throwing tons of dirt and debris high up into the air to come falling back down to earth in a bizarre rain.

"What the Sam Hill—," Carruthers yelled.

"*Duck!*" Ki warned as the debris continued falling, some of it crashing through the fringed roof of the surrey.

"Look out, Leonard!" Jessie cried and pushed Fanshaw to one side as a barrel stave, twisting end over end, crashed through the little that was left of the surrey's roof and almost struck him.

"It's the Bonanza mine," Carruthers said, leaping out of the surrey, his arms covering his head. "It's Cass Wyndman's mine."

Shouts filled the air. Cries of alarm and agony competed with them. Smoke swirled out of the tunnel leading underground. Men ran in every direction, some toward the mine entrance, others out of it and away.

Some couldn't run. One man lay not far from the mine's smoke-choked entrance, his legs twisted terribly beneath him as he raised his hands in supplication to the men passing by him and pleaded with them to help him, to take him away, to save him—*please!*

No one stopped. No one offered him aid.

Jessie, seeing the man's plight, ran to him.

"Jessie!" an anxious Ki shouted. "Come back. There could be another explosion! *Jessie!*"

She didn't pause or even slow down. She reached the man and saw that he had started to cry. Tears streamed down his cheeks to make white rivulets where they washed away some of the accumulated coal dust that begrimed his face.

"Ma'am," he cried, reaching out to Jessie. "Can you help a poor unfortunate fellow?"

"I'll do my best." Jessie bent down and put her arms around the trunk of the man's body. "When I say so, try to stand." She got a good grip on him as smoke billowing out of the mine's entrance caused her own eyes to tear. "Now!"

She got him up. But he immediately crumpled and almost took her down with him.

"My legs," the man said in a cracked voice. "Both my legs— I think they're busted. Better you should leave me, lady, lest you get caught if there's another blast. I can try crawling."

Jessie ignored him. "I'll get you away from here. Let's try again."

She hunkered down, her back to the man. "Put your arms around my neck now." When the man had done so, she braced herself and then heaved herself into an upright position. The man clung to her, his weight forcing her to walk slowly as she moved through clouds of smoke that were still pouring out of the mine. All around her men were running to and fro and shouting orders and frantic inquiries to one another.

"Did you see what happened?" one of them bellowed. "It were gas that blew!"

"I'm never going underground again!" a man vowed to no one in particular. "It's a death trap down there."

Jessie, as she continued dragging the injured miner, passed a man who was laughing hysterically and slapping his knees in a clearly inappropriate reaction to the tragedy that had just taken place.

"Pretty soon old Lucifer himself and all his imps are going to come blasting up from hell and right out into the open," she heard him cackle happily. More laughter and "Look to your immortal souls, men. Here comes the Prince of Darkness and his many black-hearted minions!"

Ki appeared out of the smoke in front of Jessie. "Let me help."

He shifted one of the injured miner's arms to his own shoulders, and then, with the man suspended between them, his legs dragging uselessly along the ground behind him, they carried him over to a grassy spot far from the tunnel leading underground and laid him down upon his back.

"Bless ye, lady," he said weakly, looking up with wet eyes at Jessie.

"You lie still," she told him. "You're safe here and there'll be a doctor along soon to take a look at you."

"Jessie—"

Ki's call didn't halt his friend, who had gone racing toward a wagon into which men had piled some of their injured comrades. When she reached it, she climbed up on the driver's seat and said, "Tell me when you're ready and I'll drive those men away from here."

"Do it now!" someone ordered her, and she promptly obeyed. She crossed a barren expanse of ground and several huge piles of tailings before bringing the wagon to a halt. She leaped from it to the ground. "Monty!" she yelled, her hands cupped around her mouth to make herself heard above the continuing din. "Leonard! Over here!"

The two men, their shirts hanging in strips and crusted blood crisscrossing their backs in ragged lines, came hurrying toward her. "Help unload these injured men," she ordered them when they reached her.

Both men hesitated and then did as they had been told.

"Was anyone killed?" Jessie asked one of the injured men as she helped Fanshaw lift him down to the ground.

"There was, yes. Oh, God, there was so *many*! Billy, he went up when the gas caught. Part of him—good God in heaven— part of him split off from the rest of poor Billy and hit me on

125

the head like a club." The man buried his face in his hands as he sat on the ground, bleeding from multiple wounds, his shoulders shaking as he wept.

Jessie, feeling heartsore and nearly helpless, left the man and continued helping to unload the injured from the wagon. In the distance, Ki was working hard to clear away rubble, together with some uninjured and only mildly injured miners, from the entrance to the mine. As Jessie worked wordlessly with several men, mules brayed occasionally but otherwise there was a terrible stillness at the scene of the explosion. No one spoke except to mutter brief instructions to one another.

It was as if the hurt and the hearty alike had been stunned by the dimensions of what had just happened. They could give it no voice; they could only stagger under its weight and try to survive.

Jessie drove the wagon, once it had been emptied of its human freight, back to pick up other injured miners. She helped load the wagon with the maimed and, in two cases, the dead bodies of miners. Soon the driving back and forth became a routine, an emotionally numbing routine. How much horror could one bear, she wondered, and still go on in the awful face of it?

She went on, her question unanswered.

She found herself some time later helping Ki and several other men push ore carts down into the black mouth of the mine, where they found more miners, many of them dead but a few still alive. They loaded both the quick and the dead into the ore carts and trundled them back to the surface.

In the long process of doing so, Jessie learned bits and pieces of information concerning the disaster. She learned that it had been caused by a gas explosion. She learned that there were miners trapped beyond a wall that had caved in when the explosion ripped apart stout timbers like matchsticks and tons of coal and earth fell to clog the mine's main tunnel. She learned that the only air shaft to vent gases from the mine had been located a half-mile away from the spot where the explosion had occurred.

She also learned that some men die with dignity and others die screaming or cursing their fate.

Nearly exhausted, she worked on beside the men, whose begrimed faces, already grim with grime, like her own she

126

supposed, grew even grimmer at the grisly discoveries they made. Bits of bodies in the rubble. A head here. A torso there. Flesh splattered in bloody masses on timbers and veins of coal.

All of it seen through the flickering light of candles and lanterns. All of it enough to make strong men cry—some did— and weaker men collapse in paralyzing shock.

When all the men had been removed that could be removed, the miners and Jessie made their sorrowful way back to the surface, pushing the last ore cart they had filled with the bodies of both the living and the dead.

They emerged into a day that had turned cloudy. Looking up at the dark sky, Jessie thought that the sun had seen enough and could look down upon the disaster no more. She wanted to close her own eyes to it as well. She wanted to turn away from it—go somewhere safe, where the world was still bright and men were not moaning and crying out in pain. But she stayed where she was, using a dipper to draw water from a wooden barrel someone had filled, and giving the water to the injured who lay on the ground or propped up against trees like badly broken dolls.

A doctor moved from one man to the next, the meager contents of his small black bag pitifully inadequate and unable to provide anything but the simplest of aid to those who needed help so desperately. She saw the stricken expression on the doctor's face as he tried his best while knowing his best was not nearly good enough. She wanted to take the man in her arms and comfort him, if such a thing were possible, and she knew it was not under the awful circumstances.

"Jessie."

Her softly spoken name seemed to come from far away. She turned. Ki was standing by her side, his hands raised as if to touch her, to offer her some tenderness.

"Ki." She had no sooner spoken his name than the tears she had held back for so long began to flood from her eyes. She stood there, her arms hanging at her sides, and wept. She wept for the dead and the dying and for those still living.

Ki tried to speak but couldn't. Instead, he reached out and enfolded his friend in his strong arms. He held her, letting her weep, feeling her body shudder against his own as the greatness of her grief savaged her.

Jessie, as she cried, could see a near mirror image of herself and Ki. Not far from where they stood, two men were standing motionless while locked in each other's arms. They were not crying. They were just standing there silently as if to hold each other harmless from the horrors abroad in the world. The poignancy of the sight, its simple beauty, tore at her heart—but also gave her hope. We suffer, she thought. But we also have strengths we did not know we had. Enough strength sometimes to help others and, in so doing, somehow help ourselves.

"Gather round, men!"

The words had been shouted by a bearded man standing on top of an overturned ore cart. He held his hands high above his head as if to draw power from the sky above him.

Jessie withdrew from Ki's embrace and, like a woman sleep-walking, moved in the man's direction, his stern and almost hypnotic gaze drawing her on.

Ki followed her, his eyes on the man he had never seen before, an uneasiness stirring within him. What was the man up to? He had a feeling that the answer might turn out to be: No good.

"Listen to me, men!" Jessie heard the man cry as she took up a position with Ki close to the ore cart. "You don't all know me, so the first order of business is to tell you my name. It's Caleb Pace."

Jessie and Ki exchanged glances, both of them recognizing the name of the labor leader who worked in Monty Carruthers's mine. A cheer went up from a few men in the crowd.

"I heard what happened here and I left work at once and came right over. I've been trying to help those of you who aren't beyond help, as are so many of the men who worked in that hellhole of a mine owned by Mr. Cass Wyndman. I regret I couldn't do more. But I can't bring back the dead. What I can do is support you in your fight to close down death traps like this Bonanza mine."

"I see a strike on the horizon, Jessie," Ki whispered.

She said nothing, her eyes on Pace, her mind almost mys-tified by the sound of his persuasive voice.

"I've come here, men," Pace continued, "to talk to you about last straws."

128

"I don't get you, Caleb," someone in the crowd called out.

"Last straws," Pace repeated, pointing a long bony finger at the man who had just spoken. "Like the one that broke the camel's back that you've all heard tell about."

The listening miners exchanged glances. They muttered among themselves. They watched Pace with awed eyes as if watching for the Second Coming or some other kind of miracle.

"This—what happened here today," Pace said, with a sweeping gesture that encompassed the entrance to the mine and the debris and mangled bodies lying about the area, "*is our last straw!*"

"Say it, Caleb!" someone shouted. "Say it loud and clear so the whole world will hear you!"

"I will, my good man," Pace promised. "What I have to say is important, and indeed the whole world should hear it as you suggest. We'll have no more of poorly ventilated mines which allow gases to build up and cause explosions like the one that happened here today to take from us so many of our brothers in misery."

"*Hold on!*" Monty Carruthers roared.

Jessie, Pace's spell momentarily broken by the two shouted words, glanced over her shoulder to where the mine owner was shouldering his way through the crowd.

"You have no proof that poor ventilation had anything at all to do with what happened here today!" Carruthers shouted when he reached the ore cart. "It was probably caused—as have been so many other similar but less deadly explosions in the past—by carelessness on the part of a miner. Somebody probably set it off by the misuse of a blasting cap."

"Do you have proof of that?" Pace yelled at Carruthers.

"Any number of things could have caused the explosion," Carruthers said, not answering the question. "A spark could have set off a blast hole that had missed fire and nobody noticed that fact."

"An act of God could have caused it," Pace mincingly mocked. "But I trust God not to do such a terrible thing. I *don't* trust Mr. Cass Wyndman. I do trust the men who told me that the buildup of gases was what did it."

"A spark—" Carruthers began.

129

But Pace interrupted him. "A spark, yes. From a miner's pick striking rock. *Carruthers, you're putting the goddam horse before the cart!* The spark didn't cause the explosion. Sure, a spark set it off. But it was the *gas buildup* that *caused* the explosion. And why did the gas build up? Because Mr. Cass Wyndman refused his miners' repeated requests to sink more vent holes to draw off gases so that such a thing as this would not happen.

"But Wyndman refused to spend the money to sink so much as a single additional air shaft. That, Mr. Carruthers, since we're talking about causes, is what brought about the explosion that killed I don't know how many good men and made I don't know how many mourning widows. I don't know how many died here today because they're still counting the corpses."

As Pace paused to catch his breath, Jessie whispered, "He's probably right."

"You think so?"

She looked at Ki. "I do."

"He's not proven his case. What he's given us so far is just a lot of rhetoric."

"Even if careless use of dynamite did cause the explosion," Pace went on, glaring at Carruthers, "which I do not believe was the culprit in this case, you mine owners could do something about that, too."

"What?" Jessie called out.

"They've got new drills on the market these days," Pace replied, shifting his gaze from Carruthers to Jessie. "They run on compressed air. If we had them to use in the mines, we wouldn't have to use dynamite anymore."

"What would happen to us drillers, Caleb, if such drills should come into use in the mines? They'd put us skilled drillers right out of work, would they not?"

"No, they wouldn't." Pace said, shaking his head. "Drillers such as yourself could be taught to use the new drills. Nobody would lose their jobs. There's also other dividends to be gained by using such machines, above and beyond the reduction of the risk of mine explosions."

"What kind of dividends are you talking about?" Jessie asked.

"You're Miss Jessica Starbuck, aren't you?" Pace asked her.
"I am."

"Miss Starbuck, I'd have thought a mine owner such as
yourself would make it your business to keep up with the latest
developments in the field of hard rock mining. Yet you profess
to know nothing about the new drills that use compressed air.
That tells me something about the degree to which you are
concerned for your employees' welfare."

Jessie was about to correct Pace, explain that she leased
her mine to Luke Hodges, who employed the men to work
it, but she held her peace on that score. Instead, she said, "I
am a woman with many business enterprises to look after,
Mr. Pace. The matter of compressed air drills has, I admit,
escaped my attention. I thank you for bringing me up to date
on the matter. Now, if you will explain what other benefits
such equipment will bring to the mining operation in this area,
I shall be obliged to you."

Pace gave Jessie a bow that was not without a faint trace
of mockery. "The exhaust from such drills, Miss Starbuck, is,
I'm told, most refreshing, and God knows the miners below
ground could use some refreshment as they toil. Then, too, air
from the lines could be used to operate blowers to cool things
down underground, where the temperatures, as you may not
know, often climb higher than one hundred degrees. The air
in the lines can also be tapped to run hoisting engines to make
our work a bit easier."

"I'll say this, Mr. Pace," Jessie called up to him. "I'll look
into this and get back to you. It may be that such drills can be
profitably used in the mine I lease to Mr. Hodges. I'll discuss
the issue with him."

"Of course you'll want to make sure that compressed-air
drills can be used 'profitably,' Miss Starbuck," Pace snarled.
"But what if it turns out that you and Hodges decide they'll
cut too deeply into your profit—their initial cost and/or cost
of operation, say? What then, Miss Starbuck?"

"She told you she'd investigate the matter, Pace," Ki said,
his tone warning Pace not to goad Jessie any more.

Pace hesitated a moment. Then, "Well and good. Did you
hear that, men? Maybe we're making some progress in at least
one of the mines around here, to better our working conditions

131

and avoid such tragedies as has needlessly overtaken us here today."

"Words are fine," a miner called out as he held a blood-soaked bandage to his wounded head, "but deeds are a whole lot better."

"Hear, hear!" someone cried.

Applause broke out in the crowd.

Pace held up a hand for silence. When the applause died away, he said, "There's only one way to make sure changes are made in the mines. That man there just said he favors deeds over words. Well, so do I, so do I, most definitely. And this is the deed I favor most right at the moment. Its name is strike."

Murmurs and mutterings spread like wildfire through the eagerly listening crowd.

"I say we walk out of every mine in the area, men," Pace continued. "I say we do not one more lick of work, any Man Jack amongst us, until the mine owners meet our demands for safer and more bearable working conditions and a rise in wages."

"We're with you, Caleb!" someone shouted.

Someone else shouted, "Let's march right now, men!"

Pace jumped down from the ore cart. Within minutes, the miners had assembled behind him. He led them away from the Bonanza mine, none of them looking back.

"Damned troublemaker," Carruthers muttered. "Well, Pace isn't going to close down my mine, by God!"

"What do you mean, Monty?" Jessie asked. "He said he intended to close down every mine in the area."

"I told you before, Jessie, when I first mentioned Caleb Pace and his threats to stir up labor trouble. I told you I'd bring in other men to work my mine if there was a strike. Men glad to do a day's work for a day's pay. That's exactly what I'm going to do.

"By the way, Jessie, I had a thought on the drive here. I plan to meet with members of the Choctaw Legislature and see if I can't get them to overturn Chief Bryant's objections to what Leonard and I are planning to do."

"You're referring to developing the coal deposits your geologists have discovered and building a spur line to serve them, I take it."

"Yes, that's exactly what I mean."

"You've already gotten permission to do whatever is necessary to develop the Choctaw coal deposits from Arthut Pryor, the Indian agent," Jessie pointed out. "Why do you need the legislature's backing?"

"Call it politics," Carruthers responded smoothly. "We could proceed without help from the legislature, but if we had that, it would strengthen our case considerably."

"Do you think the legislators will be more amenable to your plans than Chief Bryant was?" Ki inquired.

"I don't know for sure," Carruthers glumly admitted. Then, brightening, "But it's worth a try, don't you think?"

"Monty, I must say I have to admire the way you won't let things get you down," Jessie said.

"I'm a fighter, Jessie. You ought to know that by now. I'm also good at holding grudges against the likes of that Choctaw Bryant. I'll beat him at his own game before this is over, wait and see if I don't."

"It sounds to me like you're planning on doing the same thing where Caleb Pace is concerned," Jessie observed.

"And you, if I may make so bold as to say so, should do the selfsame thing to keep your mine—that is to say, Luke Hodges's mine—operating. Hire other men to work it until Pace and his flock of bleating sheep get hungry enough to come to their collective senses and return to work in the mines under conditions exactly the way they are at the present time. Now then. Are we all ready to return to town?"

On the drive back to McAlester, Jessie was silent while Carruthers and Fanshaw talked excitedly of arranging a meeting with the Choctaw legislators as soon as possible and Carruthers's decision to hire men to break the strike that would otherwise cripple his mine.

Ki, watching Jessie out of the corner of his eye as he drove the surrey back to McAlester, knew she was planning her next move, but he did not question her concerning it. She would tell him if and when she thought it was time for him to know. But he found it hard not to come right out and ask her what was on her mind, since his curiosity was aroused and, on top of that, he knew Jessie was an enterprising woman who would undoubtedly come up with a plan that was

133

both clever and innovative. He hoped it would not also be a dangerous one, as Jessie's plans and plots sometimes turned out to be.

When they reached McAlester, Ki drove to the livery and returned the rig he had rented. There, he and Jessie parted company with Carruthers and Fanshaw.

On their way back to the hotel, they heard more than one group of people excitedly discussing the disaster that had occurred earlier at the Bonanza mine. Some of the people wept openly; others hid their grief and concern beneath muttered curses and posturing bravado.

When they arrived at the hotel, they found Luke Hodges pacing the lobby. He hurried up to them and blurted out, "They've closed my mine down tighter than a drum, Jessie. Every mother's son walked out when they heard the news that Caleb Pace has called a strike as a result of the explosion at the Bonanza."

"I know," Jessie said.

"I came here to talk to you after I heard what had happened and my men left me high and dry," Hodges said, "but you weren't here."

"Ki and I were out at the Bonanza. We happened to be passing by it when the explosion occurred."

"You were on the scene? It must have been terrible, from what I hear."

"It was," Jessie said solemnly.

"What are we going to do now?" Hodges asked. "I mean now that the miners have gone out on strike?"

"Excuse me," Ki said. "While you two talk business, I think I'll get something to eat."

"I'll see you later," Jessie said. When Ki had gone, she turned to Hodges and said, "Let's sit down over there. I'm about bushed."

"If you'll forgive me for saying so, Jessie, you do look a bit shopworn," Hodges observed as they headed for a cluster of chairs in a corner of the lobby. "Your hair's in disarray and there's dirt on your face, and tell me, is that blood on your clothes?"

Jessie slumped down in one of the chairs, and Hodges sat down in one next to hers.

"Ki and I spent a few hours helping the injured out at the site of the explosion. That's where the dirt and blood came from. But I was already in poor shape when we came upon the explosion. I'd been kidnapped by some Choctaws and taken to a grove where Chief Bryant was presiding over the whipping of Monty Carruthers and Leonard Fanshaw, to, as he put it, teach them a lesson."

Jessie went on to tell Hodges what had happened in the grove, and when she had concluded her account, he reached out and gently took her hand.

"That's a terrible story. I feel like going out after Bryant and teaching him a lesson or two to pay him back for what he had done to you."

"It's over and done with now, Luke."

"Do I understand you to say that you're just going to forget all about what was done to you? Let bygones be bygones?"

"I'm not planning to retaliate in any way, if that's what you mean. But neither am I going to forget in a hurry what was done to me and, more importantly, what it means."

"What does it mean?"

"It means that the Choctaws are determined to stop us from doing business in their republic. That's their long-range goal. They've tried intimidating, as I've explained. Bryant is hoping that what happened in the grove, when it becomes public knowledge, as it surely will, will deter us from continuing to operate our mines. Ultimately, I believe, he's going to have us run out of his territory as intruders if we don't leave voluntarily."

"Well, he won't run me out. I'm no runner. I'm a fighter."

Hodges's words reminded Jessie of similar ones spoken recently by Monty Carruthers. She could see trouble lurking behind such words.

"Carruthers is going to hire strikebreakers," she told Hodges. "I don't want to follow the same course."

"You mean you don't want *me* to follow the same course."

"Yes, that is what I mean. Luke, I have no right to tell you how to operate your mine. There's nothing in our contract that gives me that right. But I ask you now to hold off on taking such action, if that is indeed what you have in mind."

135

"Jessie, I can't afford to let my mine lie idle for long. I'll go broke if I do."

"I understand your predicament, Luke. But let's give things time to settle down a bit before we do anything rash."

"Well—"

"Please, Luke."

Hodges hesitated a moment and then nodded. "All right, we'll try it your way. But I have to tell you, Jessie, I'm not going to just lie down and let Caleb Pace walk all over me forever."

"I'm going to look into the feasibility of changing some aspects of the way your mine operates, Luke. If I can figure out a profitable way to make those changes, I'll outline them for you, and if you agree they're worth putting in place, we'll do so, and I believe the result will be that the men will come back to work in your mine. If that does happen, it could be the crack in the strike armor of Caleb Pace. The entire strike structure might then crumble and things return to normal if I can also persuade men like Monty Carruthers to follow the same new procedures that will make the work of our miners both easier and safer."

Jessie got to her feet. "Now, if you'll excuse me, Luke, I think I'll turn in and get some much needed rest."

Hodges got to his feet and blocked Jessie's way as she was about to head for the stairs at the other end of the lobby. "I know you're tired, Jessie, but I had hoped when I came here today that, despite all the trouble you and I are facing, we could—Well, I suppose it was a foolish idea. Especially considering what happened to you at the hands of the Choctaws."

Jessie gazed into his yearning eyes for a moment. "It wasn't a foolish idea at all, Luke. It was, as a matter of fact, a very flattering idea. I'm pleased that you still want me even though I know I must look like something the cat dragged in."

She took his hand and led him to the stairs, which they climbed together on their way to her room.

Chapter 9

"You're sure you want to?" a concerned Hodges asked after stepping into Jessie's hotel room right behind her and taking her in his arms.

"Are you trying to back out on our deal?" she asked him teasingly.

He smiled and kissed her full on the lips. His arms went around her waist and slowly eased down until his hands were cupping her buttocks. He pulled her against him and held her there, his pelvis moving slightly in a rotating rhythm that Jessie found almost instantly arousing.

She returned his kiss with a keen intensity, surprised to find that as she did so her weariness, and the aches that had invaded so many of her muscles, and the pain that still lingered where the whip had landed on her back, all began to fade away, although they did not entirely disappear.

Hodges helped her undress, an action that she found, as she always did with him, even more arousing than his kiss. His movements were slow, almost languid. Buttons surrendered to the touch of his fingers. Buckles gave way under his touch. Articles of clothing slipped from her body to reveal the rounded curves of her hips, her pertly upthrust breasts, the slightly rounded mound of her belly, and the thatch of coppery hair growing in a V between her long, lean legs.

When he was finished disrobing her, she lay down on the bed, on her back, her arms at her sides, and watched him undress. He moved swiftly now, flinging his clothes on the floor, until he, too, was naked, his long, throbbing shaft jutting upward as desire flooded him as well.

He lay down beside her and wrapped an arm around her. She snuggled up to him, her lips brushing his cheek, his chin, the upturned tip of his aquiline nose.

She moaned with pleasure as his right hand began to explore. It sent a thrill of pleasure through her as his fingers flickered lightly over her skin. He touched and then tweaked the nipples of her breasts, and they stiffened in response. His hand finally came to rest, but only for one hot moment, on her mound, and then he was massaging it and inserting a single finger of his right hand—the middle one—into her. She couldn't help it. As if he had mesmerized her—and in a way she knew he had done exactly that with his lovely lover's touch—she raised her pelvis to meet his probing finger.

The sensations he was arousing in her made her tremble. They made her want him—desperately.

"Please," she whispered, her neck arched and her head thrown back. "Now, Luke, now!"

His finger slid out of her; his shaft slid into her. Slowly. Teasingly. He supported himself on his hands and looked down at her as he thrust and then withdrew somewhat before thrusting again.

Her body rose to meet him. Her hands encircled him and pulled him down upon her. He covered her completely, his shaft buried deep within her. She held him tightly, as if to prevent him from escaping.

But he remained a willing and even eager prisoner as he began to pound her and she matched her body's rhythm to his own.

The bed springs creaked. Hodges grunted and then moaned.

His blond hair hung down in front of his face as he raised himself slightly to watch the emotions flickering across Jessie's face—a swoon, a twist of the lips, an open-mouthed sigh of sweet pleasure. He never let up for a moment, and as a result Jessie quickly reached a body-shuddering climax.

"Luke!" she cried, clutching him to her, and "*Luke!*" again.

He exploded a moment later. As he did so, a long, drawn-out sigh escaped from between his lips. He tossed his head, and his hair flew back but then promptly tumbled down in front of his eyes again. Through it he saw Jessie as if she were slivered into sections. But the sensations he was feeling as he continued spurting within her were not splintered but entirely whole and almost overwhelming in the depth of their pleasure-giving capabilities.

"Don't," Jessie whispered, drawing him close to her as he started to withdraw.

He flopped back down upon her, drained, satisfied. He slid his hands beneath her and held her, his head turned to one side, his member still tumescent within her. Then, slowly, like a dancer performing a familiar and exciting routine, he began again to move. His buttocks rose and fell, rose and fell. His hands held her close to him. As she cried out in excitement and her fingernails clawed his back, he swiveled and twisted his hips in such a way that his erection plowed even deeper into her.

Once again his actions brought a wordless cry of delight and desire to her lips. Once again they soared together to new erotic heights. This time, they climaxed together, their bodies shaking violently. Hodges's toes curled, all ten of them, in a pleasurable tension. Jessie's body arched upward and her lips found his neck, which her teeth began to nibble.

Later, when they finally separated and lay side by side, their hands linked, Jessie whispered, "It was so good. No, it was wonderful."

"It's never like this for me with any other woman, Jessie," Hodges whispered with his eyes contentedly closed. "Only with you do I feel—I don't know what the right words are. But suffice it to say it always was and always is the best, the very best, with you."

They embraced warmly and then their lips met and held.

139

• • •

Early the next morning, Jessie knocked on Ki's door, which he opened almost immediately.

"I wasn't sure if you were up yet," she said as Ki greeted her with a smile.

"Couldn't sleep. There was a pair of demented alley cats outside last night, and they were either fighting or declaring their love for one another. Whichever it was, it kept me awake half the night. Have you had breakfast?"

"No, I was going to ask you to join me."

"Glad to."

They made their way down the stairs and were crossing the lobby when a sleepy-eyed desk clerk called out, "Miss Starbuck, one moment, if you please."

Jessie went over to the registration desk as the clerk took a folded envelope from a pigeonhole behind him and handed it to her.

"This came for you just a few minutes ago by messenger. I thought it too early to take up to you, but now that you're here . . ." He smiled as Jessie thanked him.

She opened the envelope, which was addressed to her, as she and Ki walked up the street a few minutes later. "It's from Monty Carruthers," she announced as she read the handwritten message the envelope had contained. "He's arranged a special meeting of the Choctaw Legislature for later this morning. He thought I might want to attend. He says he's planning to try to persuade the legislators to overrule Chief Bryant on the matter of who operates the mines and how."

"The man doesn't let any grass grow under his feet, does he?" Ki commented as they entered a restaurant a block from the hotel. "Yesterday he was whipped almost senseless by orders of Chief Bryant, and here he is the very next morning mounting a new challenge to Bryant's authority."

"It should be an interesting meeting," Jessie mused as they sat down at a table that was covered with a brightly checkered cloth.

A waiter came to their table, and they both ordered hearty breakfasts.

"I'd like a cup of coffee while we're waiting," Jessie told him. "Ki?"

"Tea, please."

"I persuaded Luke Hodges not to hire strikebreakers as he was inclined to do," Jessie began when the waiter had gone into the kitchen. "I think if we let things cool down a bit, maybe we can all work something out together."

"It's a ticklish problem you're facing, Jessie. It's got more angles than a man can count. Indians who want the white miners out of their territory. Miners who want more than most mine owners are willing to give them. That fellow Daniel Marshal, who wants the Choctaws to take over and operate the mines. Men like Carruthers, who wants to squeeze every cent he can out of his mines—"

"I'm going to try one more time with Monty."

"Try what?"

"To get him to hold off on working his new coal field. Maybe there's some way to patch things up between him and Chief Bryant."

"He doesn't seem interested in patching anything up," Ki remarked as the waiter brought their breakfast. "He seems more inclined to fight tooth and nail for what he wants and never mind what the chief wants."

"As I said, I'm going to try to dissuade him from that course of action—at least, for the time being. Later—Well, we'll see what develops."

They began to eat then, both of them lost in their own thoughts, and when they had finished and paid for their meals, they left the restaurant and started down the street, Jessie leading the way.

"Where are we going?" Ki asked her.

"I want to stop at the telegraph office before we head for Carruthers's office."

Ki waited outside while Jessie entered the office some minutes later, and then, when she rejoined him some time later, he asked, "Who were you wiring?"

"Dade Humboldt. You remember him, don't you?"

Ki thought for a moment. "I do. He's the executive vice president in charge of operations in Starbuck Enterprises' gold mines in Dakota Territory's Black Hills, as I recall."

"I wanted to ask him what he knew about compressed air drills, which might have some bearing on settling the miners' strike here."

They made their way through the streets to Carruthers's office and found the mine owner busily at work despite the early hour.

"Ah, Jessie, I see you got my note," he greeted her. "Good day to you, Ki."

"Monty, I came here to ask you to reconsider your decision to go ahead with your plans to develop the new coal field you've discovered."

Carruthers frowned up at Jessie from behind his desk. "You're joking, my dear."

"I'm not, Monty."

"But you can't be serious."

"I am."

"Well, I will tell you right here and now and in no uncertain terms that I intend to forge ahead. I did not go to the trouble of arranging what amounts to an emergency meeting of the Choctaw Legislature to back off now simply because you want me to. Which brings another question to mind. *Why* do you want me to back off?"

"To help keep the peace with the Indians."

"After what they did yesterday to me, to Leonard, and to you as well—you dare to come here and talk to me of peace?"

"Monty, if you won't agree to hold off, I have to tell you I've decided to speak out at the meeting in favor of not granting you the right to proceed."

Carruthers's frown deepened into a scowl. He slowly rose from his seat behind his desk. Placing his hands on his desk, he leaned over it, and, glaring at Jessie, said, "I'm warning you. If you try to hinder me, you'll live to rue the day you did."

"Monty, be reasonable."

"Get out of here. Both of you. *Now!*"

"Monty—" Jessie tried again.

Carruthers pointed to the door. *"Go!"*

Ki placed a hand on Jessie's arm, a signal. She hesitated, about to try again to change Carruthers's mind, but then thought better of it and left the office with Ki.

"Did you really mean what you said in there?" he asked her.

"I did."

"How do you suppose you can stop Carruthers?"

"I don't know. But that doesn't mean I won't try. Maybe something will come up at the legislative meeting that will help me decide. We'd better go to the town hall. The meeting's due to start soon."

"A word of caution, Jessie. My reading of Carruthers is that he's not a man to tangle with. Chief Bryant did, and look where it's getting him."

"I'm not afraid of Monty."

Jessie glanced at Ki, but he said no more as they continued on their way to McAlester's town hall.

"The purpose of this meeting today," declared a Choctaw who had introduced himself as Davis Brent to the assembled people in the meeting room of the Choctaw town hall, "is to consider whether or not to grant a charter to Mr. Montague Carruthers to mine the coal located in the southwestern quadrant of Choctaw Nation, which he has requested of this distingushed body.

"In addition, we must consider the application from Mr. Leonard Fanshaw for the right to build a spur from the Missouri, Kansas, and Texas Railroad's main line to Mr. Carruthers's planned mining operation."

"I object most strongly to both requests," declared Chief Bryant, shooting to his feet and practically shouting at Brent. "Intruders have no place in our republic."

"Chief, we must consider what is good for the tribe as a whole," Brent argued. "We have profited mightily in years past as a result of royalties collected from the mine owners you are pleased to call intruders in our land. What is wrong with profiting further from *expanded* mining operations?"

"I'll tell you what is wrong," Chief Bryant thundered. "It is wrong to exploit natural resources which belong to *us*!"

"We are not miners, Chief," a legislator pointed out mildly.

"We can learn to be, Mr. Pennington," Bryant responded quickly.

The man named Pennington smiled indulgently and said, "Can the bluebird learn to be a buffalo?"

"There is nothing innately wrong with or deficient in the Choctaw people that would prevent them from mining their own coal and mining it profitably," Bryant persisted.

Ki leaned close to Jessie, as they sat in the front row among the spectators, and whispered, "He won't go down without a fight, will Bryant?"

"If he goes down at all," Jessie whispered back.

"Chief Bryant, with all due respect," Davis Brent said, "I find your position rather unreasonable in the face of the history of coal mining in our republic. I refer, of course, to the fact that for many years white men," he bowed in Jessie's direction, "and white women have mined coal here under contracts signed with duly authorized representatives of Choctaw Nation such as yourself, Chief. What harm can come from expanding such a practice now?"

"None!" called out a man seated in the rear of the room.

Jessie glanced over her shoulder. "That's Cass Wyndman, who owns the Bonanza mine," she told Ki.

"I've mined coal in this area for four years now," Wyndman said. "Once I manage to recover from the disaster that overtook me—I refer to the explosion I'm sure you've all heard about—I intend to continue mining coal here. I will, that is, if Chief Bryant doesn't try any of his strong-arm tactics on me, with possibly fatal results. Tactics like those he recently used on my colleague Mr. Carruthers and also on Mr. Fanshaw of the Katy railroad and on Miss Jessica Starbuck."

Mutterings were heard from many of the listeners following Wyndman's gibe.

"I think," said Davis Brent, "that we all know what is at stake here and what can and must be done about it."

"Drive the white intruders out!" a Choctaw man shouted angrily.

"And then what?" Brent shot back at the man. "Let our schools suffer for want of money to buy sufficient instructional materials? Let our roads and our long-planned building program go to rack and ruin? The desperate course you suggest, sir," Brent pointedly told the man who had just spoken, "would do a disservice to all of us—most particularly to our younger generation. The bitter fruits of such shortsighted action might not be apparent all at once, but they will be in the fullness of time. But enough of this debate. I move that we put the motion before this body to a vote."

"Mr. Brent," Jessie said, getting to her feet, "I would like to make a comment, if I may."

"Certainly, Miss Starbuck," Brent said lugubriously. "As a mine owner, you have, I'm sure, pertinent things to say on this important issue."

"I would like to urge the legislature to vote down both charter applications before it."

"Miss Starbuck!" an obviously shocked Brent cried. "Surely, you don't mean what you say."

"I am not addressing the particular merits of either charter at the moment. What I am doing is urging that these charters not be approved at this particular juncture."

"But why, Miss Starbuck?" Brent inquired, his brow furrowing.

"Mr. Wyndman has just referred to the conflict that exists between Chief Bryant and his supporters on the one hand and persons like myself on the other hand."

"We have all heard what happened to you, Miss Starbuck," Brent said, "at the hands of unruly elements in our midst. Let me take this opportunity to express our dismay over the event and offer you our humblest apologies."

"I'm afraid there will be more and perhaps worse trouble if the charters are granted," Jessie continued, nodding in acknowledgment of Brent's deference to her. "I am asking a simple thing. That we all wait. That your august body not act precipitously. I am asking for time to let troubled waters become calm once again. I am asking that we sit down, all of us, and try to reason together to solve the problems that are facing us, rather than taking actions which may very well make matters worse, and quickly."

Brent hemmed and hawed for a moment, looking to the right and left at the faces of the legislators seated at the table with him. Then he said, "A call for reason to prevail is always welcome among men—and women—of good will. It most certainly is, yes."

He hemmed and then hawed some more. "But we must act. In action, I believe, lies the solution to our complex dilemma."

"But must you act now?" Jessie persisted. "A few more days won't make any difference, will it? The coal of which we speak

145

has been where it is for centuries. It can remain untouched for a few more days without anyone suffering as a result."

Jessie, as she spoke, was keenly aware of Carruthers seated across the room and giving her black looks, which, she thought, if they were daggers, would have killed her twice over by now.

Carruthers, his stern gaze still fixed on Jessie, rose to his feet. "Mr. Brent, a word or two if I may."

"Certainly, Mr. Carruthers. Proceed, please."

"I don't care, nor does it matter to anyone else here, I daresay, if the coal of which we speak has been where it is for millennia, not mere centuries. That time span is beside the point, and I don't know why Miss Starbuck has chosen to plead the coal's hoary age as a point to bolster her argument. In my opinion, it does not.

"I therefore suggest that we proceed apace. Mr. Brent, you were going to vote on my request for a charter to mine that coal, I believe. I trust that may now be done with expeditious speed."

"Wait one minute!" Jessie cried. "What is the reason for the rush to judgment here, Mr. Carruthers? Why do you feel such an urgent need to obtain your charter? Why cannot you permit others to be heard from—others who might also object, as do I, to your request?"

"Are there any objections to putting the two charter applications before us to a vote?" Davis Brent asked, scanning the faces of the spectators.

"I vote against it," the same angry Choctaw man who had spoken before bellowed.

"So do I," a man sitting next to him shouted.

Brent banged his gavel on the table to restore order. When the crowd had quieted, he said, addressing the two vociferous objectors, "You have no vote on this issue and you both know it, gentlemen. The legislators will decide this issue in a calm and considered manner."

"Calm and considered!" Chief Bryant said from where he sat with his arms folded across his chest. "You are, I submit, Mr. Brent—you and your colleagues at the table there with you—calmly considering burying our beloved Choctaw republic under the avaricious onslaught of white intruders interested

146

only in their own economic good and who are willing to let the Choctaw people be damned in the process."

A suddenly fidgety Brent turned to the right and then to the left where his fellow legislators sat. "Are we ready, gentlemen?"

"We are ready," said the gruff man to the right of Brent.

"We will do this in a fair and aboveboard manner," Brent intoned. "We will take a vote and the secretary will record it. Are you prepared to do so, Mr. Carlin?"

The secretary raised a pencil to signal that he was ready to record the vote.

Brent pointed to the man seated farthest away from him on the left. "Mr. Brown? Do you vote to approve the charter applications before us?"

"Approve, Mr. Brent."

"Mr. Metcalf?"

"Approve."

Jessie sat down in her chair as the roll call vote proceeded.

Ki glanced at her and saw the discouragement that bordered on despair in her face as legislator after legislator approved Carruthers's and Fanshaw's charter applications.

She hung her head, a symbol of defeat, as Davis Brent turned to the audience and announced, "As you have all just heard, the vote has been unanimously in favor of charter approval. I therefore and hereby declare that both charters are approved under Section Nineteen, Paragraph Four of the Choctaw Constitution."

Brent banged his gavel on the table and said, "This meeting is now adjourned."

Jessie and Ki both rose and started in silence for the door of the town hall. On the way, they passed Carruthers, Wyndman, and other mine owners who were congratulating one another on what was, judging from their statements, clearly a shared victory for all of them.

Carruthers: "I'll go and tell Fanshaw right away about the good news. He's a bit under the weather with a touch of influenza and couldn't be here today."

Wyndman: "You fought the good fight, and you won a victory for all of us, Monty. Nice going!"

Once outside, Jessie halted.

147

"What is it?" Ki asked her, seeing the firm set of her jaw and the stern look in her eyes.

"I think I'll go back inside. I would like to have a look at the part of the Choctaw Constitution under which those charters were approved."

"Why, Jessie? What possible good can that do now?"

"Frankly, I don't know that it can do any good. I suppose I just want to see for myself that the statute does indeed exist and that the wool isn't being pulled over anyone's eyes."

"You think Davis Brent and all those other legislators were pulling a fast one of some kind?"

"They may have been. I intend to make sure one way or the other. If I find that they were—Well, there's going to be a hot time in the town of McAlester."

"I suppose I shouldn't try to dissuade you from what you want to do, but I do think you're wasting your time. You're letting stubbornness override good judgment."

"Maybe so."

"Shall I wait here for you?"

"Would you mind? I won't be long."

When Jessie had gone inside the town hall building, Ki strolled across the street to look at a display of tools in the window of a hardware store. He was still gazing at them when he saw, reflected in the glass of the hardware store window, Davis Brent appear in the town hall's doorway and peer up and down the street, which was now nearly empty, since the crowd that had attended the legislators' meeting had long since dispersed.

Ki watched Brent, who seemed even more fidgety now than he had during the meeting.

Brent turned and beckoned to someone unseen before starting up the street.

The other legislators emerged from the building and hurried after him, more than one of them glancing over their shoulders now and then as if they feared being followed.

Their edgy actions intrigued Ki. He decided to follow them. Keeping to the opposite side of the street, he did so for nearly twenty minutes through the town's twisted streets. When they crossed the Katy tracks on the edge of town near the depot, so did Ki, taking care not to be seen. Up ahead of them, he saw first Brent and then the others duck into a freight warehouse situated behind the depot.

Ki went up to it and was disappointed to find that the building had no windows, so that he could not see what was going on inside from where he was. He flattened his back against the building's wall right next to the door, which was ajar, and listened to the voices drifting out of the building's dim interior. He recognized Brent's voice but not the words the man was speaking in hushed tones. He also, to his great surprise, recognized the voice of Monty Carruthers.

" . . . in hundred dollar bills," he heard Carruthers say. "Count it, gentlemen, if you like."

There was silence then.

By Ki's reckoning several minutes passed before he heard Brent say, "One thousand exactly. You've all received the same agreed-upon amount, have you, gentlemen?"

There were pleased murmurs of assent from the other legislators inside the warehouse with Brent and Carruthers.

"There's more where that came from," Carruthers promised. "Next time I need a vote from you gentlemen that favors me— I know I can count on you."

"You can," Brent assured Carruthers. "At a thousand dollars per man, we'll vote you King of Choctaw Nation should that ever turn out to be your pleasure."

"So this is how you got your unanimously favorable decision," Ki said to Carruthers as he threw wide the warehouse door and stepped inside. "You bought it."

"What are you talking about?" a flustered Carruthers boomed as he gestured to two of the Choctaw legislators who still had their share of the bribe money in their hands.

"I'm talking about that," Ki said, pointing to the folding money the two Choctaws were hastily stuffing into their pockets.

"That money," Carruthers began, "is payment for services rendered. You may not be aware that Mr. Davis Brent is a lawyer who represents me in business matters."

"And the rest of these fellas," Ki said with a sardonic smile, "I suppose they're Brent's law clerks."

"Get out of here!" Brent cried. "You are intruding, sir, on a private matter."

"I'm going to blow up your bought bonanza, Carruthers,"

Ki warned. "I heard what went on in here and I'm going to tell Chief Bryant all about it."

Carruthers apparently decided to try to brazen the matter out. "It's your word against ours," he pointed out, trying to smile.

"That might not be enough, I'll admit," Ki said. "So I'd like to let you all know that I'll need your confessions."

Carruthers laughed. "How in the world do you think you're going to get them?"

Instead of answering with words, Ki moved swiftly up to Brent. He seized the man by the shoulders, turned him, twisted his right arm up behind his back, and said, "Say it."

"Say what?" Brent cried and then screamed as Ki twisted his arm.

"Confess! Let me hear you tell the truth about what just happened."

Brent needed no further physical persuasion. He gave an elaborate confession, to the dismay of the others in the warehouse.

"I'll be back for you, Brent," Ki promised. "When I do get back, be ready to sing that pretty song again—the one you just sang for me. If you should skip town, I'll come for one of you other fellas. And if you all skip town—I'll come for you, Carruthers."

Ki left the warehouse and hurried back the way he had come, anxious to tell Jessie what he had just learned.

After she left Ki, Jessie climbed the stairs to the second floor of the town hall, where, not far from the landing, she found a glazed glass door with a single word lettered on it: Records.

She went inside and told the clerk behind the high counter, which separated the public from the private areas of the office, that she wanted to see a copy of the Choctaw Constitution.

"One moment, please." The clerk left the counter and went to a wooden file cabinet, which he rummaged through for several moments before coming up with what Jessie wanted.

He handed her the printed copy of the constitution and returned to his desk, where he began to plow through piles of assorted papers as Jessie began to peruse the document she had been given.

She ran a finger down the first page, searching for what she wanted to examine. It wasn't there. She turned to page two. It wasn't there either. She finally found it on page five.

Section Nineteen, Paragraph Four read as follows:

> Be it known by these presents that the duly appointed authorities of Choctaw Nation do hereby declare it to be the right, nay, the duty, of those in positions of power to grant charters to qualified persons who may or may not be members of the tribe, to pursue diligently and with due speed the development of any and all coal deposits found within the borders of Choctaw Nation.
>
> Let it be also known that such person or persons shall receive from Choctaw Nation any and all assistance in their endeavors within reason. It is hereby stated and affirmed by all parties to this amendment to the tribal constitution that all encouragement shall be given such person or persons and that every assistance shall be offered to facilitate their endeavors for the good of the Nation and its sundry inhabitants. Anyone attempting to interfere with this edict shall suffer not less than five or more than ten lashes.

Jessie's heart sank. She was about to summon the clerk and return the document to him, since the section and paragraph under which the legislature had acted clearly stated that the charters granted to Carruthers and Fanshaw were in perfect order according to the written law.

But then, before she could do so, something caught her eyes. She scanned the page she had been reading. She quickly flipped through the rest of the pages. She went back to Section Nineteen, Paragraph Four again. Her heart leaped as hope flooded it.

"Sir," she said, addressing the clerk.

"Yes?"

"May I ask you a question about this?" She held up the sheaf of papers in her hand.

The clerk rose and came over to the counter.

"There is a blank space here," Jessie said, pointing to one in the left-hand margin, next to Section Nineteen, Paragraph Four. "There is also a similar blank space to the left of Section

151

Twenty-one, Paragraph Two. But all the other amendments to the constitution have dates noted beside them in the left-hand margin. For example, these."

She pointed to Section Twenty, where all the individual paragraphs listed under that section bore dates, most of them from the years 1881 and 1883.

"Why are there blank spaces next to some of the amendments?" she inquired.

The clerk took the papers from her and peered nearsightedly at them. "One moment," he said. He carried the papers to his desk, found a large ledger, and opened it.

Jessie watched as he shuffled through its pages. He paused at one point. Nodded. Paused again. Nodded again.

"It is as I thought," he said after returning to the counter and Jessie. "Of course, the absence of dates could be explained away as a simple clerical oversight, but I have just checked and found that has proved not to be the case, I am naturally pleased to say. We take pride in what we do and how we do it here in the records office."

"I'm not at all sure what you're talking about," Jessie said, impatience growing within her.

"These blank spaces that you pointed out to me signify that the two amendments in question have not yet been officially ratified by the legislature."

Jessie drew in a deep breath as excitement coursed through her, and then let it out. "Would you say," she began, trying to keep her voice from trembling with the excitement she was feeling, "that these two amendments are not legally valid because of the fact that, as you have just pointed out to me, they have not yet been ratified?"

"That is correct. You see, when an amendment is ratified, notice to that effect is sent from the legislature to this office. We record the date of ratification in our ledger and then in the left-hand margin next to the amendment in question on all current copies of the constitution. As you can plainly see, there are no such marginal notes next to the two amendments you called to my attention, nor has ratification been recorded in our ledgers."

"Thank you very much. I wonder if I might take this copy of the constitution with me."

"You may upon payment of the standard purchase price of twenty-five cents."

Jessie quickly paid and then hurried out of the office and down the stairs. When she emerged from the building, she looked about for Ki, eager to tell him what she had discovered. But he was nowhere in sight.

He's probably gone back to the hotel, she thought. She hurried down the street and within a short time had reached the hotel. But when she knocked on Ki's door, there was no answer.

She made her way back downstairs to the lobby, where she asked the desk clerk if he had seen Ki. He had not.

"I'd like to leave a message for him."

The desk clerk promptly supplied her with a pencil and a piece of printed hotel stationery. She hurriedly wrote her message, folded it, and handed it to the clerk before rushing back out onto the street, where she headed for Monty Carruthers's office to confront him with what she had discovered. She could hardly wait to see the expression on his face when she revealed to him that the amendment to the Choctaw Constitution under which he and Fanshaw had been granted their charters had never been ratified, thus making both charters legally worthless.

Chapter 10

"Where is he?" Jessie demanded as she burst through the door of Monty Carruthers's office.

"Where—" The startled clerk in the outer office took a step backward. "Mr. Carruthers is in his office."

Jessie strode across the room toward the door that led to the inner office.

"But you can't go in there now!" the clerk cried, trying to block Jessie's path. "Mr. Carruthers is engaged."

"I don't care if he's engaged or married ten times over!" Jessie cried and shoved the clerk out of her way. She threw open the door and strode into the room, where Carruthers was seated behind his desk talking to two armed men who towered above it.

"What is this!" he barked as Jessie shouldered her way in among the men. "What do you want?"

Jessie pulled the copy of the Choctaw Constitution from her pocket and threw it down on the desk in front of Carruthers. "Read Section Nineteen, Paragraph Four," she ordered.

"Read— I'll do no such thing. Get out of my office. Right now!"

Jessie picked up the constitution and waved it in front of Carruthers's face. "The section under which you received your charter from the Indians has never been ratified. See here!" She pointed to Section Nineteen. "There's no date of ratification noted here. The clerk in charge of records at town hall verified for me that this section is invalid since the legislature has never voted on it."

Carruthers shot to his feet. "A mere technicality!" he bellowed. Then, to the two men ogling Jessie, he said, "Remove her from this office at once."

"You're out in the cold, Monty," Jessie said. "I'm going to the legislature with this and show them that they had no right to grant you and Leonard Fanshaw your charters the way they did. Then I'm also going to Chief Bryant and arrange to have your—and Fanshaw's—charters revoked."

"You won't," Carruthers said, his voice suddenly husky. "Hold her!"

Jessie tried to fight off the two men who seized her, but they were big and burly, and she didn't have a chance against one of them, let alone two of the broad-shouldered behemoths.

"Let me go!" she demanded, but they didn't.

"I'll see to it," Carruthers said, his eyes afire, "that the legislature rectifies their oversight. I'll see to it that Section Nineteen is ratified posthaste."

"If you do—I still won't stop fighting you," Jessie insisted. "I'll fight you at any and every turn, Monty, until you finally agree to act sensibly."

"You'll fight *nobody*!" A hectic flush suffused Carruthers's jowls. "You and that Japanese friend of yours, you're both finished. You've done your last dirty deed to me."

"Ki's got nothing to do with this, so leave him out of it. This is between you and me, Monty."

"You're wrong about that, Jessie, dead wrong. Ki's made himself a very vital part of this. A most obnoxious part, I must say."

"I don't understand."

"After the meeting of the legislature, he pussyfooted his way to a meeting I had with the legislators in a freight warehouse

155

near the depot. There he found out that I had paid those gentlemen for their very valuable services."

"Paid them?" Jessie frowned. "Are you saying you *bribed* them to vote in your favor?"

"If you wish to put it in such crude terms, yes. These men," Carruthers indicated the armed toughs, who were still ogling Jessie, "were hired by me, along with a score of others like them, to work my mine and thus help break Caleb Pace's strike. When I had the run-in with Ki, who, by the way, has also threatened to expose me, I summoned these two gentlemen to eliminate your friend so that I would not be bothered by him anymore. Now, here you are trying to make even more trouble for me. Well, it comes down to a simple matter of priorities. Instead of taking care of Ki first, these men of mine will take care of you first and Ki second."

Jessie tried to break free of the two men holding her. But even after kicking one of them in the shin, she failed to do so.

"What we just discussed in regard to the Jap," Carruthers said smoothly to his men, "do it instead to her." His finger jabbed the air, pointing at Jessie.

"But, Boss—" one of the men began uncertainly.

"What's wrong?" Carruthers snapped.

"Boss, she's a woman."

"Danvers, don't tell me you have qualms or scruples about eliminating a woman," Carruthers gibed. "All right. I'll double the fee I've agreed to pay the pair of you for the elimination of Ki to get rid of her. How does that suit you?"

"Just fine, Boss, just fine," a beaming Danvers answered.

"Then you and Bissell proceed with what we agreed upon. No, don't go out that way. My clerk is out there. Take her out the back door."

Jessie opened her mouth to scream, but before she could do so, Danvers's rough hand clamped down on her mouth to silence her completely.

No sooner had that been done than Jessie was dragged roughly across the room, bumping her hip painfully against Carruthers's desk in the process, out the back door, and down a dingy alley to she knew not where.

• • •

When Ki arrived back at the town hall and saw no sign of Jessie, he went inside and up to the records office, where he inquired if she was still there.

"No, sir," the clerk who had dealt with Jessie told him. "The lady left quite some time ago."

Once outside on the street again, Ki returned to the hotel, where he went at once to the desk clerk and asked if there were any messages for him.

"Yes, sir," the man behind the desk said cheerfully. From a pigeonhole behind him he plucked a folded piece of paper and handed it to Ki.

Ki unfolded the piece of hotel stationery and read the message Jessie had left for him.

> Ki:
>   I've found out that Carruthers's and Fanshaw's charters are invalid because the section of the Choctaw Constitution under which they were granted has never been ratified by the legislature. I'm off to point this fact out to Monty and tell him that I'm going to see to it that both charters are revoked on that basis. I'll see you shortly.
>
> Jessie

Pocketing the message, Ki returned to his room to wait for Jessie to return.

He was still waiting an hour later. Waiting and worrying. She should have returned to the hotel by now, he told himself. Perhaps she had but had not contacted him. He left his room and knocked on her door. No answer. He knocked again and called her name. Still no answer.

He returned to his room to resume waiting for her.

When more anxious minutes had passed and she still had not put in an appearance, he left the hotel and headed for Carruthers's office.

"Where's your boss?" he asked Carruthers's clerk when he arrived at his destination.

"In his office. Have you an appointment with him?"

"Tell me something," Ki said, ignoring the question. "Did a lady come here to talk to him this afternoon?" He described Jessie to the man.

"Yes, sir, she was here. And very rude she was, I must say."

"Rude?"

"She burst into Mr. Carruthers's office before I could stop her."

"Is she still in there?"

"Oh, my, no."

"When did she leave?"

"I don't know that, sir. She left with the two gentlemen who had come to call on Mr. Carruthers. By the back door. So I didn't see them leave. But when I next entered Mr. Carruthers's office, some time after the lady arrived here, all his visitors were gone."

Ki headed for the door that led to the inner office.

"Sir, please!" the clerk called distractedly. He leaped up from his stool, but he was too late to prevent Ki from entering Carruthers's office unannounced.

"I'm looking for Jessie Starbuck," he announced without preamble to a startled Carruthers. "I was told by your clerk that she was here and then left with two men. Where did she go? Do you know?"

"I do not," Carruthers answered bluntly.

"Who were the two men and why did she leave with them?"

"They were acquaintances of mine. She left with them. That is all I know. I do not know why she left with them."

"Mr. Carruthers, were you asleep during her visit here?"

"Of course not. Whatever do you mean?"

"If you were wide awake, how come you don't know what transpired here in this office that led her to leaving with those men?"

"I told you I don't know."

"And I'm telling you, Carruthers, that I don't believe a word you've said to me. Jessie has been gone for hours. She left a message for me in which she said she was coming here. She said she expected to see me shortly. She said nothing whatsoever about going off with two strangers."

"Perhaps the men weren't strangers to her. Perhaps she knew them. Besides, what does 'shortly' mean? To some women of my acquaintance 'shortly' means hours."

Ki swiftly rounded Carruthers's desk. He seized a fistful of the man's shirt and hauled him up out of his chair. With his own face only inches away from Carruthers's, he muttered, "You're going to start telling me the truth, Carruthers, or I'm going to bounce you off that wall behind you. What happened in this office when Jessie came here?"

"Nothing happened!"

Ki slammed Carruthers into the wall, striking the man's head against it.

Carruthers cried out in pain.

Ki repeated what he had done and then promptly repeated it again.

Carruthers struggled to free himself from Ki's iron grip but failed to do so. Ki's free left hand seized Carruthers's throat and began to squeeze. He watched Carruthers's face turn blue. He saw the man's tongue protrude from between his lips and his eyes begin to bulge.

"When you're ready to tell me the truth about what happened here today with Jessie and those two men, I'll let you breathe, not a second before. When you want to confide in me, nod your head."

Carruthers gagged. Spittle slid from between his quivering lips.

Ki waited, wondering how long Carruthers could hold out.

Seconds later, Carruthers nodded his head.

Ki immediately released his hold on the mine owner's throat but not his hold on his shirt. "Tell me."

Gagging and spluttering as he clutched at his throat, Carruthers managed to mutter, "My mine—they took her there."

"What mine? Where?"

"I own an abandoned underground coal mine outside of town. They took her there. They work for me, those two men. I hired them to kill you. Jessie came here threatening to expose me and my machinations just as you had done earlier today. Instead of sending those men out to kill you as I had originally planned to do, I had them take her away to be disposed of. Then I intended to send them after you."

Ki swore colorfully. "Let's go."

"Where?" a now ashen-faced Carruthers asked, still clutching his throat, on which red imprints of Ki's fingers remained.

"You're going to show me this mine of yours you're talking

about before anything happens to Jessie. If it already has, you and those hired killers of yours—you're all dead men, I promise you. Now, *move!*"

Danvers and Bissell dragged Jessie, whom they had gagged, down the steeply sloping incline into the bowels of Carruthers's abandoned mine.

Danvers held high a lighted lantern in his free left hand as they made their way still deeper into the black maw of the mine.

Around them were leaning timbers and timbers that had fallen and were no longer supporting the roof of the tunnel, which was composed of hard rock mixed with coal. Ore carts sat silently on rusted iron rails. The skeleton of a mule lay in a white heap at the entrance to a side tunnel.

They rounded a cage that sat on the floor of the tunnel, with its cable running straight up a shaft into utter blackness and the now-silent hoisting works somewhere above.

"This is far enough," Danvers said. "Give me the dynamite."

Bissell shoved Jessie to one side, causing her to fall. He took several sticks of dynamite from his pocket and handed them to Danvers, who proceeded to bind them together with a ragged piece of twine. From his pocket, he took several small tubular copper blasting caps, which he handled gingerly as he inserted them into the sides of each of the sticks of dynamite that composed the lethal bundle in his hands.

"What's your hurry?" Bissell asked him. "We don't have to blow the place sky-high right this very minute, do we?"

Danvers gave his companion a questioning glance. He saw the leer on Bissell's face and the way the man licked his lips as he stared at Jessie, who lay on the ground by his boots.

"What exactly have you got in mind, Bissell?"

"A party, that's what I've got on my mind. What say we have at her before we blow this place to kingdom come?"

"The boss didn't say anything about raping her. He just wants her killed."

"What the hell do I care what Carruthers said," Bissell snapped. "Besides, he's not going to know whether we dipped our wicks in her before we killed her. Even if he did know, he wouldn't give a good goddam, now would he, do you reckon?"

Danvers looked from Bissell to Jessie. "She's a pretty package, ain't she?" he said speculatively.

"*De*lectable," Bissell enthusiastically agreed. "Tell you what, you can go first. I don't mind standing in a short line like we've got here for a go at her."

Jessie got to her feet and attacked Bissell. Her fists flew, landing on the man's face and on his body. She clawed. She scratched. She pummeled Bissell.

Danvers grabbed her from behind and threw her to the ground.

Bissell began to unbutton his trousers.

"No," Danvers said in a cold voice.

"What do you mean, 'no'?"

"I mean we came here to do a job and we're going to do it."

"Ah, come on, Danvers. Don't be such a spoilsport."

As the two men continued to argue, Jessie scanned the area. If she could somehow manage to escape from them—get away to a place she could hide and from which she could then find her way to the surface despite the darkness . . .

She decided to chance it. She ran, ripping the gag from her mouth and throwing it away. Within minutes, she was in utter darkness, which was filled with the sound of the pounding footsteps of the two men who were pursuing her. She ran on, colliding with a tunnel wall at one point, which made her left shoulder ache and tore her blouse.

Behind her, flashes of light illuminated the darkness. They climbed the walls, swung this way and then that, as the lantern in Danvers's hand bounced about. She used her hands to feel along the tunnel wall. She found what she at first thought was a small side tunnel, into which she darted. But a feeling that was close to despair nearly overcame her when she discovered that the tunnel was not a tunnel at all but merely a gouged-out space in the wall, where miners had picked away at a layer of coal. Nevertheless, she huddled on the ground, trying to melt into the wall as the light of Danvers's lantern speared the darkness, disappeared for a moment, and then speared it again. She held her breath as the two men came closer to her hiding place.

She let her breath out in a rush when they had run past the alcove where she crouched, and then she sprang to her feet, intending to retrace her steps and find, she hoped, the tunnel leading upward to the surface.

"Where'd she go?" Bissell shouted, his voice echoing in the darkness.

"We must have missed a cutoff somewhere," Danvers said. "We'll go back the way we came."

Danvers and Bissell began to retrace their steps.

Jessie, hearing the pair returning, abandoned her plan to make a run for it in the dark. She remained where she was, hoping they would not find her hiding place. If they did— She wouldn't let herself think about that. As she sat huddled against the rear wall of her refuge, she thought about what she had heard the two men say Carruthers wanted done with her, as they drove in a wagon to the mine. They intended to dynamite one wall of the mine to let the river that flowed nearby flood it.

She shuddered. According to Danvers, Carruthers, who had planned this fate for Ki originally, didn't want any, as he called them, "inconvenient bodies" showing up to start people asking questions and making inquiries. Ki would have been—and now she was on the verge of being—drowned in a flooded mine, never to be seen or heard from again.

Ki viciously whipped the team of horses he was driving as the surrey he had rented in town tore along the road and Carruthers, seated beside him, held on for dear life.

"How much farther?" Ki yelled above the din of the horses' pounding hooves.

"Just up there around that bend!" Carruthers yelled back.

Moments later, the surrey rounded the bend on two wheels and the gaping entrance to the mine yawned blackly in the side of a hill.

Ki drove up to it, brought the team to a snorting halt, and shoved Carruthers out of the carriage. He grabbed the lantern he had brought, leaped down to the ground, seized the mine owner by the arm, and began to sprint toward the mine entrance.

Huffing and puffing, Carruthers could barely keep up with him.

Ki lit the lantern and started down into the mine, still holding tightly to Carruthers.

"No!" Carruthers cried, trying to hold back from entering the mine. "If the dynamite goes off, we'll be blown to bits!"

Ki never faltered. He continued dragging Carruthers down into the mine, the light of his lantern sending shadows scurrying here and there. He passed the empty ore carts and the skeleton of the long-dead mule lying beside them. He raced past the empty cage that had once carried men to and from the building that housed the hoisting works far above.

He came to a tunnel that intersected at a right angle the one he was in. "Which way now?" he asked aloud, addressing the question to both himself and Carruthers.

"They would have gone to the left," Carruthers answered. "The river's over that way."

Ki hustled his prisoner to the left, ignoring the sound of Carruthers's whimpering, which verged on outright weeping. He had not gone far when he heard the sound of approaching footsteps. He halted, listening.

"This way!" he heard a male voice call out. "She's over here somewheres. I heard her!"

Moments later, light danced into view and then so did the lantern that was being held high in Danvers's hand. "What the hell?" he exclaimed when he caught sight of Ki and Carruthers.

Ki stepped behind his prisoner and pinioned the man's arms behind his back.

"What's going on, Boss?" a startled Bissell asked as he moved into sight from behind his partner.

"This is the man I hired you to kill. He's got no gun. *Kill him!*"

Bissell drew his revolver and took aim at Carruthers, behind whom Ki was standing.

"Not *me!*" Carruthers cried. "Him! Kill *him!*"

"How the hell can I," Bissell yelled, "if you don't get out of the way?"

Carruthers kicked backward, his foot catching Ki in the shin and making him lose his grip. Carruthers broke away from him and went racing toward the other two men in the tunnel. Within seconds, he was cowering behind Danvers.

Bissell, chuckling at the smoothness of his maneuver, raised his gun and took aim at Ki. His fingers tightened on the trigger.

It was then that Jessie appeared behind the trio who were facing Ki.

Ki kept his face expressionless in order not to betray her presence behind the three men. He watched her raise the large chunk of coal she had in her hands and then bring it crashing down on Carruthers's head.

The man dropped like a stone.

Jessie used the coal as a club to strike Danvers, who also went down but did not lose consciousness as Carruthers had.

Bissell whirled and fired a snap shot that missed Jessie by little more than an inch. Before he could fire at her a second time, Ki jumped him. The two men fell to the ground and rolled over.

Jessie had moved close to them, looking for a chance to brain Bissell with the coal in her hands, when Carruthers suddenly regained consciousness, seized the gun Bissell had dropped when Ki jumped him, and yelled, "Back off or she dies!"

Ki froze at the shouted command. Then, warily watching Carruthers's shaky gunhand, he released Bissell, who got to his feet and kicked him in the ribs.

"Good going, Boss!" Danvers cried, also getting to his feet. "You got the drop on both of them."

"Now I want them both dead," Carruthers muttered. "Maybe this time you can do it right."

"What went wrong, Boss, was—"

"I don't want to hear it. Shoot them both. Then we'll light the fuses and get the hell out of here."

Bissell thumbed back the hammer of his revolver as Danvers took the bundle of dynamite from his pocket and began inserting fuses into each individual stick.

"Well, what are you waiting for?" Carruthers snarled.

"Back up, Jessie," Ki whispered.

As both of them quickly did, Bissell snickered. "They look like two frightened rabbits about to make a run for it, Boss." He raised the barrel of his gun and took aim at Jessie, a mirthless smile on his face.

Ki, judging that the distance between him and Jessie and the three co-conspirators was now sufficient, came to a halt. So did Jessie.

Before Bissell could fire, Ki suddenly dropped to the ground. When he came up an instant later, he had filled both of his hands with coal dust, which he flung in Bissell's face, blinding the man.

"Run, Jessie!" he yelled.

As she turned and ran, Ki sprang to his feet, took a *shuriken* from his pocket, and threw it. The five-bladed star spun end over end as it flew through the air, and then it struck one of the blasting caps Danvers had inserted in the dynamite he was holding in his hands.

As the dynamite exploded with a bright flash of orange fire and a thunderous roar, Ki was thrown to the ground. But he immediately sprang to his feet and went running in the direction Jessie had taken, glancing over his shoulder as he did so.

It was hard to see, but he saw enough to make him shudder before thick smoke billowed through the tunnel and engulfed him.

"Ki, where are you?" Jessie called from somewhere in the blackness.

"Here," he called back. "Keep talking, Jessie, so I can find you."

"I'm here. This way. Can you hear me?"

"Keep talking."

Jessie did. Her words and the sound of her coughing led Ki to her. After embracing her, he asked, "Are you hurt?"

"Shaken up but not hurt. What about you?"

"I'm all right. I got hit with some flying debris, but it's nothing serious."

"How are we going to get out of here? The blast has blocked the tunnel." Jessie guided Ki's hands to the pile of timber and rock that blocked their escape from the tunnel. "Maybe we can dig our way through it," she suggested tentatively.

When Ki drew away from her, she asked, "Where are you? What are you doing?"

"Looking for a way out."

Ki felt along the tunnel wall and soon came to a dead end. He started in another direction and stumbled over something in his path. It turned out to be the skeleton of the dead mule. He remembered it and the ore carts near where it lay. He also

165

remembered the cage and the cable on top of it that led to the hoisting works on the surface. He quickly began to search for the cage, hoping and praying that it had not been destroyed or buried by the explosion.

He found it a few minutes later. He ran his fingers along the cage's slatted sides and then climbed to the top of it, where he was relieved to find that the cable remained intact. He called to Jessie, "We have a chance to get out of here."

"How?"

"I'm on top of the cage. It's cable leads to the hoisting works. We can try climbing it."

For a moment, Jessie was silent. Then Ki heard her moving toward him as he spoke her name again and again to help guide her to him.

When he heard her below him, he reached down. "Can you find my hand?"

She did, after a moment of fumbling about in the utter darkness, and Ki pulled her up onto the top of the cage with him.

"Now, you'll go first," he told her. "I'll be right behind you. Are you ready?"

He guided her hands to the many twisted wires that made up the thick cable and waited as she began her hand-over-hand climb in the smoky blackness that surrounded them both.

When she was several yards above him, he also began to climb the cable.

Time passed slowly. A time of aching muscles and sweat and relentless exertion on the part of both of them. Then Jessie's voice, weak and unsteady, reached Ki where he clung to the cable below her. "I don't think I can hold on any longer. I'm losing my grip!"

Ki quickly climbed another few feet. "Stand on my shoulders and rest for a few minutes." He reached up with one hand and guided Jessie's feet to his shoulders. Then he held tightly with both hands to the cable as he supported her, both of them motionless.

"I'm better now," she said a few minutes later. "I think I can make it now."

"Give it the best shot you can," he told her as he felt her feet leave his shoulders and she resumed her arduous climb.

For a time there was only the sound of their ragged breathing in the shaft they were slowly ascending. There were moments when Ki thought he was going to lose his grip on the cable. But he managed to hold on. So did Jessie. Then, after what seemed like an eternity, Jessie cried, "I can see light above me!"

Her words sparked an even greater effort in Ki. He climbed as fast as he could, holding back only once, when Jessie paused to get her breath. Then she stepped out onto the rotting wooden floor of the hoisting works, which was filled with the huge silent shapes of the rusting hoisting engine and the gigantic wooden spool on which the metal cable was wound.

Ki emerged from the shaft a moment later to find Jessie slumped on the floor and breathing harshly. He joined her, and they sat together in silence for several minutes.

Then, Jessie asked, "Carruthers—he died down there?"

"Him and his two hired killers did, yes."

"You saw what happened to them?"

"They were blown to bits. It wasn't a pretty picture."

Nausea rose in Jessie's throat, threatening to overwhelm her as ghastly pictures of the fate the three men had met flooded her mind.

"Do you think you can make it outside now?" Ki asked her.

When she nodded, he helped her up and out of the hoisting works into the orange light of a sunset that seemed more beautiful than any either of them had ever seen.

Jessie and Ki stood on the depot platform talking to Luke Hodges as they waited for the southbound train that would take them home.

"I wish we'd have another miners' strike," Hodges declared.

"Luke!" Jessie exclaimed. "I wouldn't wish that on my worst enemy. Whatever made you say a thing like that?"

"If we had a strike," Hodges said, winking at Ki, "you'd stay on here awhile longer and help settle it as you did the one that just ended."

Jessie smiled.

"I still don't know how you did it, Jessie. To get all the mine owners to agree to increase the daily wage from three to four dollars."

"She did it," Ki said, "with a skillful mixture of good business sense and feminine wiles."

"The thing that really brought Caleb Pace and the other striking miners around," Jessie said, "was the introduction in your mine, Luke, of those water-flushed drills I learned about from Dale Humboldt."

"You should have seen Pace's face when Jessie first announced that they were going to be used in her mine and all the other mines in the area," Ki told Hodges. "He had taunted her earlier for not being aware of compressed-air drills, and then she turned around and wired Humboldt for information about them, and he told her about the water-flushed drills, which easily top the older compressed-air drills. Her move knocked his pride down a peg or two."

"Those new drills are terrific," Hodges said. "They're sure to cut down on the dust that causes Miner's Consumption. It plagues the men who work in the mines."

"Jessie also helped take Leonard Fanshaw down a peg or two just as she did Pace," Ki pointed out. "The Nation's going to let him build all the spur lines he wants—if he pays the tribe a dollar-and-a-half per foot of track. That fee was her suggestion."

"Jessie," Hodges said, "I want to thank you sincerely for what you did in regard to the new royalty arrangement you made with Chief Bryant. If I had to pay additional cents on top of the one cent I already pay per ton to the tribal treasury, it would make things tough for me. So the fact that you, as mine owner, have agreed to pay the increase in my share of the royalty rate is a mighty big help to me."

"Chief Bryant was as pleased as Punch," Jessie said, "when I persuaded the other mine owners to go along with the increase in the per-ton royalty rate. Oh, they grumbled about it, but in the end they went along."

"Maybe they feared facing a similar fate to the one that brought Carruthers and his pair of gunslicks down," Ki offered facetiously.

Jessie frowned. "Let's not talk about what happened to those men. Every time I think of it, I'm horrified all over again."

"They deserved what they got," Hodges declared vehemently. "When *I* think of what they tried to do to you and Ki—"

168

"The train's coming," Jessie said, interrupting Hodges.

"Jessie," Ki said, "there's one thing I'm uncertain about. Did Chief Bryant and Daniel Marshal ever agree about what should be done with the higher royalties they will now be collecting from the coal mines?"

"No. The last I knew, they were still arguing about how that money should be used. But thank heaven they did finally agree with the representatives of the mine owners and the miners themselves that they should not take over and try to run the mines themselves. They're content, they now say, to let others grub in the muck for the money that they then sit back and share without ever having to get their hands dirty."

"Not to mention not having to risk getting killed in the doing of the job," Hodges stated.

His next words were drowned out by the train as it rumbled into the station, sparks flying from the rails as the iron wheels ground to a halt.

"Good-bye, Luke," Jessie said, going to him and giving him a warm embrace and a kiss on the cheek. "It's been good seeing you again."

"I hope next time it will be under far better conditions."

"I hope so, too. Although *all* the conditions under which we met this time were not what you could call disagreeable, don't you agree?"

Ki smiled to himself as Hodges began to blush, and then Ki and Jessie carried their luggage aboard the train and waved good-bye through the window as the train chugged out of the station, heading south.

GILES TIPPETTE

Author of the best-selling WILSON YOUNG
SERIES, BAD NEWS, and CROSS FIRE
is back with his most exciting
Western adventure yet!

JAILBREAK

Time is running out for Justa Williams, owner of the Half-
Moon Ranch in West Texas. His brother Norris is being held in
a Mexican jail, and neither bribes nor threats can free him.

Now, with the help of a dozen kill-crazy Mexican *banditos*,
Justa aims to blast Norris out. But the worst is yet to come:
a hundred-mile chase across the Mexican desert with fifty
federales in hot pursuit.

The odds of reaching the Texas border are a million to nothing . . . and if the Williams brothers don't watch their backs,
the road to freedom could turn into the road to hell!

Turn the page for an exciting preview of
JAILBREAK by Giles Tippette

On sale now, wherever Jove Books are sold!

At supper Norris, my middle brother, said, "I think we got some trouble on that five thousand acres down on the border near Laredo."

He said it serious, which is the way Norris generally says everything. I quit wrestling with the steak Buttercup, our cook, had turned into rawhide and said, "What are you talking about? How could we have trouble on land lying idle?"

He said, "I got word from town this afternoon that a telegram had come in from a friend of ours down there. He says we got some kind of squatters taking up residence on the place."

My youngest brother, Ben, put his fork down and said, incredulously, "*That* five thousand acres? Hell, it ain't nothing but rocks and cactus and sand. Why in hell would anyone want to squat on that worthless piece of nothing?"

Norris just shook his head. "I don't know. But that's what the telegram said. Came from Jack Cole. And if anyone ought to know what's going on down there it would be him."

I thought about it and it didn't make a bit of sense. I was Justa Williams, and my family, my two brothers and myself

175

and our father, Howard, occupied a considerable ranch called the Half-Moon down along the Gulf of Mexico in Matagorda County, Texas. It was some of the best grazing land in the state and we had one of the best herds of purebred and crossbred cattle in that part of the country. In short we were pretty well-to-do.

But that didn't make us any the less ready to be stolen from, if indeed that was the case. The five thousand acres Norris had been talking about had come to us through a trade our father had made some years before. We'd never made any use of it mainly because, as Ben had said, it was pretty worthless because it was a good two hundred miles from our ranch headquarters. On a few occasions we'd bought cattle in Mexico and then used the acreage to hold small groups on while we made up a herd. But other than that, it lay mainly forgotten.

I frowned. "Norris, this doesn't make a damn bit of sense. Right after supper send a man into Blessing with a return wire for Jack asking him if he's certain. What the hell kind of squatting could anybody be doing on that land?"

Ben said, "Maybe they're raisin' watermelons." He laughed.

I said, "They could raise melons, but there damn sure wouldn't be no water in them."

Norris said, "Well, it bears looking into." He got up, throwing his napkin on the table. "I'll go write out that telegram."

I watched him go, dressed, as always, in his town clothes. Norris was the businessman in the family. He'd been sent down to the University at Austin and had got considerable learning about the ins and outs of banking and land deals and all the other parts of our business that didn't directly involve the ranch. At the age of twenty-nine I'd been the boss of the operation a good deal longer than I cared to think about. It had been thrust upon me by our father when I wasn't much more than twenty. He'd said he'd wanted me to take over while he was still strong enough to help me out of my mistakes and I reckoned that was partly true. But it had just seemed that after our mother had died the life had sort of gone out of him. He'd been one of the earliest settlers, taking up the land not long after Texas had become a republic in 1845 I figured all the years of fighting Indians and then Yankees and scalawags and carpetbaggers and cattle thieves had taken their toll on him. Then a few years back he'd been nicked in the lungs by a bullet that should never have been allowed to head his way and it had thrown an extra strain on his heart. He was pushing seventy and he still had plenty of head on his shoulders, but mostly all he did now was sit around in his rocking chair and stare out over the cattle and land business he'd built. Not to say that I didn't go to him for advice when the occasion demanded. I did, and mostly I took it.

Buttercup came in just then and sat down at the end of the table with a cup of coffee. He was near as old as Dad and almost completely worthless. But he'd been one of the first hands that Dad had hired and he'd been kept on even after he couldn't sit a horse anymore. The problem was he'd elected himself cook, and that was the sorriest day our family had ever seen. There were two Mexican women hired to cook for the twelve riders we kept full time, but Buttercup insisted on cooking for the family.

Mainly, I think, because he thought he was one of the family. A notion we could never completely dissuade him from.

So he sat there, about two days of stubble on his face, looking as scrawny as a pecked-out rooster, sweat running down his face, his apron a mess. He said, wiping his forearm across his forehead, "Boy, it shore be hot in there. You boys shore better be glad you ain't got no business takes you in that kitchen."

Ben said, in a loud mutter, "I wish you didn't either."

Ben, at twenty-five, was easily the best man with a horse or a gun that I had ever seen. His only drawback was that he was hotheaded and he tended to act first and think later. That ain't a real good combination for someone that could go on the prod as fast as Ben. When I had argued with Dad about taking over as boss, suggesting instead that Norris, with his education, was a much better choice, Dad had simply said, "Yes, in some ways. But he can't handle Ben. You can. You can handle Norris, too. But none of them can handle you."

Well, that hadn't been exactly true. If Dad had wished it I would have taken orders from Norris even though he was two years younger than me. But the logic in Dad's line of thinking

177

had been that the Half-Moon and our cattle business was the lodestone of all our businesses and only I could run that. He had been right. In the past I'd imported purebred Whiteface and Hereford cattle from up North, bred them to our native Longhorns and produced cattle that would bring twice as much at market as the horse-killing, all-bone, all-wild Longhorns. My neighbors had laughed at me at first, claiming those square little purebreds would never make it in our Texas heat. But they'd been wrong and, one by one, they'd followed the example of the Half-Moon.

Buttercup was setting up to take off on another one of his long-winded harrangues about how it had been in the "old days" so I quickly got up, excusing myself, and went into the big office we used for sitting around in as well as a place of business. Norris was at the desk composing his telegram so I poured myself out a whiskey and sat down. I didn't want to hear about any trouble over some worthless five thousand acres of borderland. In fact I didn't want to hear about any troubles of any kind. I was just two weeks short of getting married, married to a lady I'd been courting off and on for five years, and I was mighty anxious that nothing come up to interfere with our plans. Her name was Nora Parker and her daddy owned and run the general mercantile in our nearest town, Blessing. I'd almost lost her once before to a Kansas City drummer. She'd finally gotten tired of waiting on me, waiting until the ranch didn't occupy all my time, and almost run off with a smooth-talking Kansas City drummer that called on her daddy in the harness trade. But she'd come to her senses in time and got off the train in Texarkana and returned home.

But even then it had been a close thing. I, along with my men and brothers and help from some of our neighbors, had been involved with stopping a huge herd of illegal cattle being driven up from Mexico from crossing our range and infecting our cattle with tick fever which could have wiped us all out. I tell you it had been a bloody business. We'd lost four good men and had to kill at least a half dozen on the other side. Fact of the business was I'd come about as close as I ever had to getting killed myself, and that was going some for the sort of rough-and-tumble life I'd led.

178

Nora had almost quit me over it, saying she just couldn't take the uncertainty. But in the end, she'd stuck by me. That had been the year before, 1896, and I'd convinced her that civilized law was coming to the country, but until it did, we that had been there before might have to take things into our own hands from time to time.

She'd seen that and had understood. I loved her and she loved me and that was enough to overcome any of the troubles we were still likely to encounter from day to day.

So I was giving Norris a pretty sour look as he finished his telegram and sent for a hired hand to ride it into Blessing, seven miles away. I said, "Norris, let's don't make a big fuss about this. That land ain't even crossed my mind in at least a couple of years. Likely we got a few Mexican families squatting down there and trying to scratch out a few acres of corn."

Norris gave me his businessman's look. He said, "It's our land, Justa. And if we allow anyone to squat on it for long enough or put up a fence they can lay claim. That's the law. My job is to see that we protect what we have, not give it away."

I sipped at my whiskey and studied Norris. In his town clothes he didn't look very impressive. He'd inherited more from our mother than from Dad so he was not as wide shouldered and slim-hipped as Ben and me. But I knew him to be a good, strong, dependable man in any kind of fight. Of course he wasn't that good with a gun, but then Ben and I weren't all that good with books like he was. But I said, just to jolly him a bit, "Norris, I do believe you are running to suet. I may have to put you out with Ben working the horse herd and work a little of that fat off you."

Naturally it got his goat. Norris had always envied Ben and me a little. I was just over six foot and weighed right around one hundred and ninety. I had inherited my daddy's big hands and big shoulders. Ben was almost a copy of me except he was about a size smaller. Norris said, "I weigh the same as I have for the last five years. If it's any of your business."

I said, as if I was being serious, "Must be them sack suits you wear. What they do, pad them around the middle?"

He said, "Why don't you just go to hell."

After he'd stomped out of the room I got the bottle of whiskey and an extra glass and went down to Dad's room.

It had been one of his bad days and he'd taken to bed right after lunch. Strictly speaking he wasn't supposed to have no whiskey, but I watered him down a shot every now and then and it didn't seem to do him no harm.

He was sitting up when I came in the room. I took a moment to fix him a little drink, using some water out of his pitcher, then handed him the glass and sat down in the easy chair by the bed. I told him what Norris had reported and asked what he thought.

He took a sip of his drink and shook his head. "Beats all I ever heard." he said. "I took that land in trade for a bad debt some fifteen, twenty years ago. I reckon I'd of been money ahead if I'd of hung on to the bad debt. That land won't even raise weeds, well as I remember, and Noah was in on the last rain that fell on the place."

We had considerable amounts of land spotted around the state as a result of this kind of trade or that. It was Norris's business to keep up with their management. I was just bringing this to Dad's attention more out of boredom and impatience for my wedding day to arrive than anything else.

I said, "Well, it's a mystery to me. How you feeling?"

He half smiled. "Old." Then he looked into his glass. "And I never liked watered whiskey. Pour me a dollop of the straight stuff in here."

I said, "Now, Howard. You know—"

He cut me off. "If I wanted somebody to argue with I'd send for Buttercup. Now do like I told you."

I did, but I felt guilty about it. He took the slug of whiskey down in one pull. Then he leaned his head back on the pillow and said, "Aaaaah. I don't give a damn what that horse doctor says, ain't nothing makes a man feel as good inside as a shot of the best."

I felt sorry for him laying there. He'd always led just the kind of life he wanted—going where he wanted, doing what he wanted, having what he set out to get. And now he was reduced to being a semi-invalid. But one thing that showed the strength that was still in him was that you *never* heard him complain. He said, "How's the cattle?"

I said, "They're doing all right, but I tell you we could do with a little of Noah's flood right now. All this heat and no

180

rain is curing the grass off way ahead of time. If it doesn't let up we'll be feeding hay by late September, early October. And that will play hell on our supply. Could be we won't have enough to last through the winter. Norris thinks we ought to sell off five hundred head or so, but the market is doing poorly right now. I'd rather chance the weather than take a sure beating by selling off."

He sort of shrugged and closed his eyes. The whiskey was relaxing him. He said, "You're the boss."

"Yeah," I said. "Damn my luck."

I wandered out of the back of the house. Even though it was nearing seven o'clock of the evening it was still good and hot. Off in the distance, about a half a mile away, I could see the outline of the house I was building for Nora and myself. It was going to be a close thing to get it finished by our wedding day. Not having any riders to spare for the project, I'd imported a building contractor from Galveston, sixty miles away. He'd arrived with a half a dozen Mexican laborers and a few skilled masons and they'd set up a little tent city around the place. The contractor had gone back to Galveston to fetch more materials, leaving his Mexicans behind. I walked along idly, hoping he wouldn't forget that the job wasn't done. He had some of my money, but not near what he'd get when he finished the job.

Just then Ray Hays came hurrying across the back lot toward me. Ray was kind of a special case for me. The only problem with that was that he knew it and wasn't a bit above taking advantage of the situation. Once, a few years past, he'd saved my life by going against an evil man that he was working for at the time, an evil man who meant to have my life. In gratitude I'd given Ray a good job at the Half-Moon, letting him work directly under Ben, who was responsible for the horse herd. He was a good, steady man and a good man with a gun. He was also fair company. When he wasn't talking.

He came churning up to me, mopping his brow. He said, "Lordy, boss, it is—"

I said, "Hays, if you say it's hot I'm going to knock you down."

He gave me a look that was a mixture of astonishment and hurt. He said, "Why, whatever for?"

181

I said, "*Everybody* knows it's hot. Does every son of a bitch you run into have to make mention of the fact?"

His brow furrowed. "Well, I never thought of it that way. I 'spect you are right. Goin' down to look at yore house?"

I shook my head. "No. It makes me nervous to see how far they've got to go. I can't see any way it'll be ready on time."

He said, "Miss Nora ain't gonna like that."

I gave him a look. "I guess you felt forced to say that."

He looked down. "Well, maybe she won't mind."

I said, grimly, "The hell she won't. She'll think I did it a-purpose."

"Aw, she wouldn't."

"Naturally you know so much about it, Hays. Why don't you tell me a few other things about her."

"I was jest tryin' to lift yore spirits, boss."

I said, "You keep trying to lift my spirits and I'll put you on the haying crew."

He looked horrified. No real cowhand wanted any work he couldn't do from the back of his horse. Haying was a hot, hard, sweaty job done either afoot or from a wagon seat. We generally brought in contract Mexican labor to handle ours. But I'd been known in the past to discipline a cowhand by giving him a few days on the hay gang. Hays said, "Boss, now I never meant nothin'. I swear. You know me, my mouth gets to runnin' sometimes. I swear I'm gonna watch it."

I smiled. Hays always made me smile. He was so easily buffaloed. He had it soft at the Half-Moon and he knew it and didn't want to take any chances on losing a good thing.

I lit up a cigarillo and watched dusk settle in over the coastal plains. It wasn't but three miles to Matagorda Bay and it was quiet enough I felt like I could almost hear the waves breaking on the shore. Somewhere in the distance a mama cow bawled for her calf. The spring crop were near about weaned by now, but there were still a few mamas that wouldn't cut the apron strings. I stood there reflecting on how peaceful things had been of late. It suited me just fine. All I wanted was to get my house finished, marry Nora and never handle another gun so long as I lived.

The peace and quiet were short-lived. Within twenty-four hours we'd had a return telegram from Jack Cole. It said:

182

YOUR LAND OCCUPIED BY TEN TO TWELVE MEN STOP
CAN'T BE SURE WHAT THEY'RE DOING BECAUSE THEY
RUN STRANGERS OFF STOP APPEAR TO HAVE A GOOD
MANY CATTLE GATHERED STOP APPEAR TO BE FENCING
STOP ALL I KNOW STOP

I read the telegram twice and then I said, "Why, this is crazy as hell! That land wouldn't support fifty head of cattle."

We were all gathered in the big office. Even Dad was there, sitting in his rocking chair. I looked up at him. "What do you make of this, Howard?"

He shook his big, old head of white hair. "Beats the hell out of me, Justa. I can't figure it."

Ben said, "Well, I don't see where it has to be figured. I'll take five men and go down there and run them off. I don't care what they're doing. They ain't got no business on our land."

I said, "Take it easy, Ben. Aside from the fact you don't need to be getting into any more fights this year, I can't spare you or five men. The way this grass is drying up we've got to keep drifting those cattle."

Norris said, "No, Ben is right. We can't have such affairs going on with our property. But we'll handle it within the law. I'll simply take the train down there, hire a good lawyer and have the matter settled by the sheriff. Shouldn't take but a few days."

Well, there wasn't much I could say to that. We couldn't very well let people take advantage of us, but I still hated to be without Norris's services even for a few days. On matters other than the ranch he was the expert, and it didn't seem like there was a day went by that some financial question didn't come up that only he could answer. I said, "Are you sure you can spare yourself for a few days?"

He thought for a moment and then nodded. "I don't see why not. I've just moved most of our available cash into short-term municipal bonds in Galveston. The market is looking all right and everything appears fine at the bank. I can't think of anything that might come up."

I said, "All right. But you just keep this in mind. You are not a gun hand. You are not a fighter. I do not want you going anywhere near those people, whoever they are. You do it legal and let the sheriff handle the eviction. Is that understood?"

He kind of swelled up, resenting the implication that he couldn't handle himself. The biggest trouble I'd had through the years when trouble had come up had been keeping Norris out of it. Why he couldn't just be content to be a wagon load of brains was more than I could understand. He said, "Didn't you just hear me say I intended to go through a lawyer and the sheriff? Didn't I just say that?"

I said, "I wanted to be sure you heard yourself."

He said, "Nothing wrong with my hearing. Nor my approach to this matter. You seem to constantly be taken with the idea that I'm always looking for a fight. I think you've got the wrong brother. I use logic."

"Yeah?" I said. "You remember when that guy kicked you in the balls when they were holding guns on us? And then we chased them twenty miles and finally caught them?"

He looked away. "That has nothing to do with this."

"Yeah?" I said, enjoying myself. "And here's this guy, shot all to hell. And what was it you insisted on doing?"

Ben laughed, but Norris wouldn't say anything.

I said, "Didn't you insist on us standing him up so you could kick him in the balls? Didn't you?"

He sort of growled, "Oh, go to hell."

I said, "I just want to know where the logic was in that."

He said, "Right is right. I was simply paying him back in kind. It was the only thing his kind could understand."

I said, "That's my point. You just don't go down there and go to paying back a bunch of rough hombres in kind. Or any other currency for that matter."

That made him look over at Dad. He said, "Dad, will you make him quit treating me like I was ten years old? He does it on purpose."

But he'd appealed to the wrong man. Dad just threw his hands in the air and said, "Don't come to me with your troubles. I'm just a boarder around here. You get your orders from Justa. You know that."

Of course he didn't like that. Norris had always been a strong hand for the right and wrong of a matter. In fact, he may have been one of the most stubborn men I'd ever met. But he didn't say anything, just gave me a look and muttered something about hoping a mess came up at the bank while I was gone and then see how much boss I was.

But he didn't mean nothing by it. Like most families, we fought amongst ourselves and, like most families, God help the outsider who tried to interfere with one of us.

A special offer for people who enjoy reading the best Westerns published today. If you enjoyed this book, subscribe now and get ...

TWO FREE

A $5.90 VALUE—NO OBLIGATION

If you enjoyed this book and would like to read more of the very best Westerns being published today, you'll want to subscribe to True Value's Western Home Subscription Service. If you enjoyed the book you just read and want more of the most exciting, adventurous, action packed Westerns, subscribe now.

Each month the editors of True Value will select the 6 very best Westerns from America's leading publishers for special readers like you. You'll be able to preview these new titles as soon as they are published, FREE for ten days with no obligation.

TWO FREE BOOKS

When you subscribe, we'll send you your first month's shipment of the newest and best 6 Westerns for you to preview. With your first shipment, two of these books will be yours as our introductory gift to you absolutely FREE, regardless of what you decide to do. If you like them, as much as we think you will, keep all six books but pay for just 4 at the low subscriber rate of just $2.45 each. If you decide to return them, keep 2 of the titles as our gift. No obligation.

Special Subscriber Savings

When you become a True Value subscriber you'll save money several ways. First, all regular monthly selections will be billed at the low subscriber price of just $2.45 each. That's

WESTERNS!

at least a savings of $3.00 each month below the publishers price. Second, there is never any shipping, handling or other hidden charges—Free home delivery. What's more there is no minimum number of books you must buy, you may return any selection for full credit and you can cancel your subscription at any time. A TRUE VALUE!

Mail the coupon below

To start your subscription and receive 2 FREE WESTERNS, fill out the coupon below and mail it today. We'll send your first shipment which includes 2 FREE BOOKS as soon as we receive it.